The Strangeness

SUDDEN FICTION

TOM NUGENT

Copyright © 2011 Tom Nugent

All rights reserved. No part of this book may be reproduced in any form by any electronic or mechanical means (including photocopying, recording, or information storage and retrieval) without permission in writing from the publisher.

Requests for permission to make copies of any part of this work should be mailed to:

Elysian Detroit
279 East Ferry Street
Detroit MI 48202

or by email to
david@mikiko.net

or by phone to
(313) 355-0696

Library of Congress Control Number: **2011938065**

ISBN: **978-1-4663090-5-0**

Printed in the USA

TABLE OF CONTENTS

9	I Am the Summer Wind
13	Twenty Questions for Modern Man
17	The Rains Will Wash Us Clean One Day
21	A Lesson from the Zen Guy
25	Quantum Thriller
29	At the Big K
33	The Flying Shitstorm
37	A Burning Question
41	Mr. Glass Eye
45	A Life-Changing Epiphany
49	The Blood of the Mosquito
53	Crystal Radio
57	What Was That? Was That a Gunshot?

One Is Necessary, One Is a Piece of Fate	61
My Name Is Frank Dempsey	65
The Aliens Have Landed	69
Waiting for The Call	73
Everything Here Eats Something Else	77
Our Invisible World	81
The Singing Fish	85
Among the Jellies	89
Strangeness	93
Family Trouble	97
Encounter with a Fire-Snorting Bull	103
Sisyphus Loves The Rock	107
I Started Breathing Very Fast, In the Car	111
Oodle-Doodle! Oodle-Doodle!	115
Birds Are Descended From Dinosaurs	119
Sometimes Making Something Leads to Nothing	125

129	The Halberd-Bearer
133	Two Guys In a Car
137	Summer Ghost, Nag's Head
141	A Mystery Story In 22 Paragraphs
145	Damaged Fruit
149	Tiny Gildersleeve
153	Among the Ojibwas
157	Down on the South Skunk River
161	Big Al's Moment of Compassion
165	Still Life With Dung Beetle
169	This Is A Red Line Train To Howard
173	Getaway!
177	Comforting Mr. T

I AM THE SUMMER WIND

Something happened on this river, about 11 years ago.

A girl got carried away. Well, it was more like driven *under*. The river was swollen, spring melt, and she tried to raft it on a green-plastic raft, and things went terribly wrong. She got pinned in a deep spot, and the raft got hung up against a stack of logs with her caught underneath, and the current held everything there for a few minutes, just long enough to take her from us.

There used to be a wooden sign at the river's edge: *We love you, Patti!*

But the years have been passing, of late. They're like the river – they just keep on going by you, slow and steady and fast, all at the same time.

She is, she was, she isn't anymore. Many of the people who knew her then have moved on, too. Her older sister Belle... she lives down in Texas now. She married a guy who works in an oil company office outside Houston. Last I heard, they had a couple of kids already in school.

I ate lunch with her at the high school, Kenmore Heights, during our junior year.

She told us how she was really hot for Brad Pitt. But of course, that was back when Brad was younger. I hear he's balding now and wearing a hairpiece.

She worked down at the Wendy's, too, after school. You'd pull up to the drive-in window and there she'd be, big as life and wearing a great big *Smile!* Button and taking your order on the speakerphone:

"Hello! Welcome to Wendy's! Have you tried our new Chicken Jubilee Fresh Fruit Salad? Please place your order when ready!"

It's strange. The months turn into years and the river keeps on running through town. The porch light goes on... and a big old spackled moth starts bumping his head against the yellow bulb. A flurry of leaves rises from the pavement, blows through your headlights.

That time Patti was among us – I want to know where that time is *now*. Does it still exist somewhere? Is there a place where she's still chattering away on Wendy's speakerphone?

I dreamed of her raft one time. This must have been a year or so after she died. I dreamed the green plastic, like a great big puffed-up plastic doughnut, and she was stretched out on it and wearing these enormous red sunglasses, and the raft drifted past me on the riverbank, and her soft blonde hair rippled against the breeze.

I tried to call out to her:

"Patti!"

"Patti!"

But no sound emerged. Nothing but air rushed from between my lips, and try as I might, I could not give that air a voice.

So I stayed behind.

The raft disappeared around the next bend. I was alone. I watched the leaves on the weeping willow go rustling away from my breath, and for a moment I understood: *I am the summer wind.*

TWENTY QUESTIONS
FOR MODERN MAN

1. If he was so smart, why did Sigmund Freud snort up all that cocaine?

2. We know that ants communicate via chemical odors... but do they translate those odors into ant "thoughts" – or only into ant "feelings"?

3. How should we picture quarks, if we want to get a realistic picture of quantum mechanics?

4. Does the fact that no future civilization has ever traveled back through time to help us solve our problems prove that our species will vanish before such a civilization can be born... or does it simply prove that time-travel is impossible?

5. Whatever happened to the joy people once felt when they pressed Silly Putty against comic strips and then lifted the cartoon images from the page... before bending and stretching them grotesquely by pulling on the Putty?

6. When our ancestors painted wild animals on the walls of caves 25,000 years ago, did they get to erase and "redo" animals they got wrong... or were they only given a single shot at each cave painting?

7. Are today's birds dinosaurs... or are they simply a new kind of animal that the dinosaurs *became* over millions of past years?

8. Whatever became of Alan Ladd?

9. Do antibiotics kill germs by depriving them of oxygen... or simply by cutting them up with specially designed, extremely sharp molecules?

10. Could atomic escaping radiation produce giant ants powerful enough to take over the New York City subway system?

11. Is our world merely a holographic projection on a "cosmic soap bubble"... or is the jury still out on that theory?

12. If the 1950s radio program *The Great Gildersleeve* is eventually listened to by sentient beings in a distant galaxy, what will the listeners make of Gildersleeve's troublesome nephew, Leroy?

13. Do tropical leaf-cutter ants know they're farmers?

14. Now that former U.S. President Gerald Ford has gone to his final reward, should we feel remorseful about all those times when we joked that he "couldn't walk and chew gum at the same time?"

15. If we find the Higgs Boson, do you think the discovery will change your daily routine?

16. Are historical events (Booth shoots Lincoln at Ford's Theatre, for example) over forever once they've

taken place... or do they continue to occur again and again, *but only in their own time*?

17. Did Julius Caesar really say "Et tu, Brute?" when he was stabbed... or did somebody make that up later because it was a terrific sound bite?

18. If squirrels didn't have cute, fuzzy tails, wouldn't every public park in America be crawling with hideous-looking rodents?

19. Isn't money simply the basic tool we use to push each other around?

20. If Freud was high on coke day after day, how come everybody now believes in the reality of the human unconscious?

THE RAINS WILL WASH US CLEAN ONE DAY

On Beaver Island, I visited an Ojibwa medicine man named Blackbird. He was a chunky guy who wore his glossy black hair in two thick braids. During one of our conversations, the healer pointed out that he never talked on the telephone.

"The phone is not so good," said Blackbird. "Phone turn you into the ghost of yourself. Make you dry up and then you blow away on the wind."

I thought about these statements for a minute. I'd just gotten off a jetliner from Los Angeles. "How do you become a ghost, Blackbird?"

He sent me a wan smile. "You talk on a wire and then you turn into electricity. Zzzzzttt! That's all you are now – a red spark on the wire. You can't even *smell* the man you're talking to."

I blinked slowly at him. I could tell that he regarded me as a ghost – a pale, northern fellow who'd been driven mad by Thomas Edison and Henry Ford.

"Blackbird," I said, "this may seem like a strange question... but what is the true nature of human reality?"

He smiled again. "Reality? I would say that spirits rule the land of the living. When you are walking in the forest and a snake crosses your path – at that instant you have been warned. Or a red-tailed hawk turns in the air. He screams at you: 'Don't take that path!'"

I mulled this notion for a few seconds. "Blackbird, do you think there's a Hell?"

He shook his head. "No Hell, Noonan – but there is a dead world. When you land a rocket on the moon, and you don't ask permission of the Moon Goddess... let me tell you, the penalty for that is the dead world."

He ran a hand along one of his braids. "NASA," he said. "This is the ruler of the dead world. Here men drink from the river... but the water runs through their fingers and they are never satisfied."

I groaned. "I'm screwed, Blackbird."

"I know," he said.

"They ate my brain."

"Yes," he said. "You wake up one day and the birds are silent."

"When I write about the Ojibway in the Detroit *Free Press* – what should I say, Blackbird?"

He considered my question for a few seconds. Then: "You could say that a remnant lives on. That we still honor our sacred sites. That the oil spills cannot hurt those who still pray at the sites."

I thanked him. "I'll try to work that in."

He took my hand. "You ask too many questions," he said. "Just remember: The rains will wash us clean someday. Now follow my truck – we go to Dairy Queen!"

I did as he instructed. We drove slowly along the island's one paved road. The pale moon hung like an ivory-hued lantern above the waters of Mich-ee-goo-mee. Now and then a shadow-winged moth would flutter through the medicine man's headlights.

About a dozen Indians had gathered on the Dairy Queen parking lot. They were all leaning against their pickup trucks and eating ice cream with white plastic spoons. The moon glowed above the ice cream stand as if powered by very strong batteries. The medicine man ordered a Cherry-Berry Split with M&M sprinkles... and he refused to let me pay for it.

A LESSON FROM THE ZEN GUY

I was feeling a tad down, what with the economic bust-out and such, so I went to see the Zen Guy. He lives behind a Chinaman's furnace on East 57th Street.

"Zen Guy, good morning."

"Uh-huh," he told me. "That's right. I'm eating a cracker." He held it up. "Do you see this cracker?"

"I do."

"Learn from it," said the Zen Guy. "What kind of cracker are we talking about, kemo sabe?"

I meditated. "Saltine?"

He grinned. "Not a bad guess. Actually, it's a Krispy."

"All right," I said. "A Krispy. I see no problem."

"Good, good," said the Zen Guy. "It's Saturday morning in New York City. Beyond that, everything is speculation. Do you have an issue?"

I thought for a minute. "I'm afraid of so many things, Zen Guy. I'm afraid something will jump out and hurt me. Something large, and probably green."

He nodded. "I hear that kind of concern quite often. Are you afraid of being bitten, voyager?"

I stared at him. "Damn," I said. "You are reading my thoughts. I fear the teeth on the green thing. Do you think I might have been traumatized, growing up?"

The Zen Guy chuckled. "You're growing up right now," he said. "You're a child at this moment, but in another place. I'm sure you understand that time doesn't exist. Time is a *place*, dear heart. Get over it."

I nodded. "I'm afraid there will be a shortage of cash," I told him after a bit. "I'm afraid I'll be forced out into the weather as a result, and I won't be able to pay for my medication. Snow will pile up on my eyebrows. No more Coney Island dogs with chopped onion and bright yellow mustard on the boardwalk.

"Honestly, I'm afraid something green will jump out of the Dipsty Dumpster and bite my abdomen."

The Zen Guy sent me his wisest smile. "Golly gee," he said, "but you do sound like a 'fraidy cat."

I had to agree. "You've called it, Zen Guy. I'm scared all the damn time. That's why I suspect early trauma. I think a black spider may have worked me over in the cradle, and I mean a big one."

He chuckled again. "Man," he told me happily, "I'm really enjoying this, okay? Here's my thought: If you run out of money, you can stay with me. Fair deal? You can live on the other side of the furnace. There's plenty of room over there and I'll give you a Krispy from time to time." He sent me a cheerful wink. "Have I helped your cause, hombre? Have I eased any of your travail?"

Instead of answering, I took his hand. I shook it. "Thank you, Zen Guy. I'm back on the beam, and you're the reason why."

He was reaching for his Krispy box. "Take a cracker," he said. "Shit, take two – they're small. And remember to keep exhaling. You'd be surprised how many people forget that."

Soon I was back out on 57th Street. I walked west for a couple of blocks. I knew that three guys might be moving a refrigerator at that moment, 40 stories above my head. They're lugging it past a big open window – and right at this moment, one of *'em steps on a roller skate.*

Aw... shit!

The fridge topples through the window and here it comes, 400 pounds of glass and steel in a thriller produced and directed by Isaac Newton. And there goes my head.

But hey... that's mere speculation. And I'm not going there. I'm going to keep on walking, that's all. I'm going to nibble on my cracker and do some significant exhaling. Okay by you?

Did a big black spider jump on this little guy?

QUANTUM THRILLER

> *In this interpretation of quantum mechanics, every event is a branch point; the cat is both alive and dead, irrespective of whether the box is opened, but the "alive" and "dead" cats are in different branches of the universe, both of which are equally real, but which cannot interact with each other.*
>
> –From the Wikipedia entry on "Quantum Mechanics"

The door of Room 409 swung open, and the card-players looked up from their hands. Their eyes jumped with amazement. *What the hell is this?*

The new arrival was a fat man carrying a nickel-plated gun.

Nobody moved.

"Okay," said the newcomer, "you boys cleaned me out last night, but now I'm back. And I've brought my two friends along – Mr. Smith and Mr. Wesson."

He pointed the dark snout of the Smith & Wesson .38 at each man in turn. There were five of them at the table, and their eyes were very large.

"You boys hoodwinked me," said the gunman. "You took my money and you laughed. You said: 'Fatso got a lesson tonight; we fucked him good.'"

Nobody moved. The radio was playing a Golden Oldie, *It's Over*, by the long-dead American blues crooner Roy Orbison.

They listened for 15 or 20 seconds to the wailing of his lonesome guitar. Then one of the men at the table raised his hand. He was a slender fellow with a bristly, nicotine-stained mustache.

"Look here, Farabaugh. It was a joke. Okay? Harmless fun. We were pulling your leg, that's all. We were gonna call you tomorrow, give you your dough back. Don't worry, we never planned to keep it. It was all a joke. We just wanted to see how you'd react. For God's sake, it was harmless fun!"

Slowly, the fat man shook his head. Then he snuffled wetly. Did he have a head cold? Or had he been weeping as he rode up in the hotel elevator? "A joke," he said softly. "Harmless fun. I don't think so. I think you were playing for keeps, hombres. And that's exactly what I intend to do."

They heard the metal *clack* of a round sliding into the chamber. Roy Orbison crooned on, slow and easy: *It's over*. It had begun to rain a little; behind the music, they could hear the slow patter of rain on window glass. It was a moment, that's all. Rain, cards, ice melting in the glasses of whiskey, sorrow from Roy Orbison.

And then the fat man took them out, one by one.

***

And then the fat man surprised them by lifting the gun to his own temple. "Don't worry, I'm not going to shoot you," he said. "Let's see if you can laugh at *this*, boys." And the gun flashed once.

***

And then the fat man dropped the pistol onto the thick beige carpet. He turned away. He started toward the door. Then he looked back over one shoulder. "You boys had you a real good laugh last night... but tonight it was *my* turn. Haw!"

And then the fat man

And then the fat man

AT THE BIG K

Thornhill went down hard, right next to *girls' apparel*. The linoleum squares rushed toward him – black-white, black-white, BAM! – and at first he assumed that he'd been shot. He was an American, after all.

His left arm, just below the elbow? A hole of fire had opened there, a black hole ringed with glowing embers – a mouth of fire was eating his arm!

No. It was something else. Wow, Thornhill told himself. This is probably a heart attack, bopper. This is probably a situation at the Big Kmart.

By now his two eyes had gone their separate ways. The left saw only black. Was that eye dead? The other one had focused on a bulb-headed little guy in funky sneakers. The bulb-head was sky-blue, and grinning, and Thornhill saw that it was pointing to a group of words printed in white:

discover
> *the easy*
> *way to pay*
> *Kmart layaway*

Thornhill tried to make sense of these white words, and got nowhere. But then a balding angel arrived. His round head glowed with soft, milky light... and his eyeglasses winked silver, winked golden in the pooling fluorescence.

Thornhill read a pale orange sign over the angel's shoulder: *plus size*. With his remaining eye, he studied the movements of the angel's mouth.

Can
> *you*
> *hear*
> *me,*
> *sir?*

Thornhill tried to respond, but the wires were down. He could not say, "Don't let them get my Jeep," try as he might. Instead of making words, he growled tenderly... and it occurred to him that words were nothing but little bursts of air pushed around by your tongue. And your tongue was... a slab of soft red meat. And your brain knew how to move that meat, how to twist and turn it and curl it back upon itself... and it was this movement, this bending and shaping that converted the growling into the words on the Kmart sign:

visit our
> *garden shop*

But the angel was singing to him now, crooning at him the way a mother croons to soothe her troubled babe: *we've called for help, sir, so just hang on.*

And Thornhill nearly smiled, because it had occurred to him that you could put those words to music, stretch them into a melody:

we've called
> *for help, sir, O yes, we have!*
> *we've called for*
> > *helllllllppppp!*
(So
> *just...*
> > *hang...*
> > > *on!)*

Thornhill wanted to applaud. He watched the radiance sparkle, flicker around the angel's eyes. How strange it was, on an ordinary Thursday afternoon, to discover that nothing... or rather everything... *Bopper*, he told himself in music rather than in words, *you did the right thing, you came to the right place, you came to the Big K!*

The angel was smiling at him. Thornhill tried to say thanks. He tried to open his mouth. He tried to –

THE FLYING SHITSTORM

I'm talking primordial *ooze*, my friends!

Can you handle that?

It's a summer afternoon, deep in the burbling precincts of the Dismal Swamp. Look at that tar-black water slopping against the cypress knees. There's something cooking under that gunk, you can be sure of it. There's a monstrosity being hatched down there – a yellow-green horror with 18 toes and a curving snout.

Trust me: creepy things are at work full-time in the swamp muck.

And there will be consequences. It may take 40 or 50 million years, but I can promise you this: More than a few of the descendants of those creepy things will eventually wind up living in New Orleans. They will dip their jumbo-sized shrimp in pungent sauces, and they will drink all manner of fiery beverages that will inspire them to earn lengthy prison time.

Trust me: This world of ours, which seems so solid and predictable and safely routine – well, it *ain't*.

Nossir.

Do you want an example?

Okay... one afternoon about 25 years ago, I was sitting in a bar in the Greektown section of Baltimore arguing about whether or not Elvis was secretly murdered. I was talking to a laid-off steamfitter... well, I never knew his actual name; everybody in the bar just called him "Mouth."

"They killed Elvis," said Mouth. "They made it look like he died of a stroke in the crapper, straining to get one out – but I read a thing in the *National Examiner*, or maybe it was the *Tattler*, said they iced that boy to get his gawd-damn *in*-surance. Elvis was heavily *in*-sured, did yuh know that? The King had at least five million on his gawd-damn head, accordin' to the Tattler."

I watched Mouth shift his giant buttocks on the stool in order to pass wind. Then I opened my yap to tell him "that's ridiculous," but I was cut short.

Pow!

Everybody stood up.

"What the shit," said Mouth. "That there was a gawd-damn gun."

For once, he was right.

We heard some high-pitched screams coming from the Ladies Room... and a moment later, two of the bartenders were pounding on the door.

More shouting... another scream, but weaker this time. Half a minute passed, and then the two bartenders emerged. They were carrying a blonde-haired woman between them, a platinum-blonde, and she was running with blood. It was just pooling off her, these great big crimson sheets of it drenching the linoleum. One of the bartenders shouted: "Need a belt – tourniquet!"

***

What had happened, the platinum-blonde had dropped her purse in the can. She'd been carrying a little 20-caliber in there, and when it hit the floor, it shot her in the thigh. Hit an artery, and she damn near bled to death before the ambo guys could reach her.

"Gawd-damn," said Mouth later. "Ain't that something? You stop off at the Athens Bar for a Bud and a little bit of gab... and instead you get the flying shitstorm!"

A BURNING QUESTION

With the passage of the years, Mullen's life had come down to a single, burning question.

Should he dig up the priest's bones and then piss on them – or not?

Mullen's 40-year-old daughter, Innocent, found the question increasingly irksome, however. "Come on, Dad, think it *through*," said Innocent. "Would you really feel any better afterward? Don't you realize... it would simply be some urine on some bones?"

And Mullen would invariably reply: "Yes, Innocent, I hear you. Still... I like the fact that it would be my urine and *his* bones!"

Mullen hated the dead priest because of the way he'd always insisted on things. The *padre* had been unrelenting, when it came to theological matters. "There's a nasty devil, all right," Father O'Toole had warned all the kids in second grade, "and we must be very careful to avoid his snares."

On one occasion, however, the seven-year-old Mullen had raised his hand.

"What is it, young man?"

"Father O'Toole... what if there really *isn't* a devil? What then?"

The priest had called Mullen's parents – and they'd blistered the young man's butt for him. Mullen's Mom had also told him: "If you ever question Father O'Toole again, don't bother to come back here, because we won't open the door to you."

After that, young Mullen sat motionless in religion class, starting straight ahead.

Fifty years later, he often found himself hanging out at the local Tru-Value Hardware on Saturday afternoons, pricing shovels.

***

Mullen had a friend, McCorkle, and one afternoon at Moriarity's, Mullen asked his pal about the advisability of disinterring the prelate and peeing on him.

"Okay, let me get this straight," said McCorkle. "You're asking me if you should dig up a dead priest in the cemetery and then urinate on his remains. Is that the basic question here?"

"You've pinpointed it," said Mullen.

"Well," said McCorkle. "Have you thought about the legal ramifications?"

"Huh?"

"Jaysus, Mullen!" McCorkle wiped foam from his upper lip. "Do you think you can just dig people up without repercussions? My God, man, where are your brains?"

"What?" said Mullen. "Is digging up the dead a crime, then?"

"Crime? *Crime*? It's a fookin' felony, boyo. It's serious shit. You'd spend ten or fifteen years in prison if they caught you."

Mullen stared at him. "Piss on a few bones and spend the next decade behind bars? I never imagined the penalty might be that severe." He thought for a minute. "You took a course in business law a while ago, didn't you, McCorkle? What would you recommend?"

McCorkle meditated for a few seconds. Then: "Thank God you've decided to be responsible and adult about this, Mullen. And I do think I have a reasonable solution. Rather than digging the priest up, why don't you just slip into the cemetery on a dark night and piss on his grave? You're far less likely to be arrested, that way... and the urine would probably seep down into his bones as an added bonus."

Mullen nodded. Suddenly, his eyes were sparkling with joy. "Bingo!" he said. "That's it! Hey, I can't thank you enough, McCorkle. Wait 'til I tell Innocent about this. She'll be so relieved to hear that I've decided to resolve the issue in such a thoughtful, mature manner!"

MR. GLASS EYE

Here's my problem, in exactly six words: I don't know what anything is.

Do you?

That old man with the glass eye and the wooden cane: what *is* that old man?

He wanted a paper bag. He growled at the cashier at Jack's Deli: "I said I want a goddam paper *bag*."

The cashier wailed back at him: "I'm sorry, sir, but I'm not allowed to give the bags away – not without a purchase."

The old man's jaw began to work. His stubbled jaw... and the gray flesh hanging beneath. The bones beneath that jaw were grinding, grinding – *rage* moved those bones. His whole life... balked!

Now he rose up to his full height. He lifted the brown cane... would he strike her with it? No. But he did point it at her. "I *made* a purchase," he roared. "I just drank a cup of the swill you call coffee. That was my purchase... and now I want my bag."

She gave in.

He tucked the little paper sack – Jack's Deli – into his coat pocket. I watched his mouth open, close, open again. I could hear him making these little sucking sounds... he was sucking air through his dentures. *This is horrible, horrible*, I thought. *Life is grotesque, terrifying, without meaning.*

He stamped past my table. He stamped along and on every other step, the brown cane smacked against the linoleum tiles of the deli.

Smack!

Our eyes met... and with a surge of green-edged horror, I found myself peering intently into the glass one. That orb was dead, inert... but then I saw a bit of light wink from it. His jaw was still working, grinding away, and his scowl ran 20,000 feet deep. Had he just arisen from the Black Lagoon... a brine-dripping sea monster draped with yellow-green weed and vomiting a torrent of half-digested squid?

I looked into the glassine silence of his petrified gaze, and once again the enigma of being rose before me: *I don't know what anything is.*

What was it the Nietzscher had said, only a few days before he snapped his tether and ran bellowing down the *Strasse* en route to permanent, shrieking, total madness?

"You must learn to love your fate," the Nietzscher had intoned while gnawing at his enormous, carpet-sweeper mustache, "for the sea will cast it up again!"

The Strangeness

Fate! A moment later, I was on my feet and hurrying after the enraged old man with the glass-dead eye. *Deeper*, I told myself, *you must plunge deeper into the strangeness*.

All at once my task seemed clear. I would follow this elderly curmudgeon at a discreet distance. I would find out where he lived. Perhaps I would knock at his door, while pretending to be a salesman or a building inspector or a city repairman come to fix the underground pipes. I would question Mr. Glass Eye carefully. I wanted to know who he was. And now, as I pushed through the big swinging doors that fronted Jack's Deli, I could make out his hunched, cane-swinging figure about 20 yards ahead. He was hurrying along, muttering to himself and from time to time whacking the brown cane against the sidewalk.

A few flakes of wet snow went sailing past. The streetlights had come on by now; they shimmered fitfully through the winter twilight.

What is everything? Could Mr. Glass Eye help me answer that question?

We walked south onSt. Paul Street, while the darkness of the approaching night slowly engulfed us.

MR. Glass Eye   **To Be Continued**

A LIFE-CHANGING EPIPHANY

O'Donnell fell out of his swivel-chair, ka-*plooey*!

He went face-down on the carpet. He lay there, snoring loudly and seemingly content.

It was Tuesday afternoon, around three o'clock, in the downtown offices of Fidelity & Liberty.

Mrs. Pennington reached him first. "Ed, are you all right?" She pulled at one of his shoulders. Nothing. She made a loud, groaning sound, like a grievously wounded sheep. "I can't... I can't get a *response*!"

I leaned over and muttered into Ackerman's ear: "He's totally shit-faced."

"Won't somebody call nine-eleven?" wailed Mrs. Pennington.

"It might be better to call *Seven*-Eleven – and then order up a six of Bud," I muttered at Ackerman.

Mr. Nolan, the regional sales manager, was kneeling on the carpet now. He had one hand on O'Donnell's chest. "Ed, are you okay? Are you okay?"

Mrs. Pennington glared fiercely at Mr. Nolan. "How can he be okay? He's lying on the carpet!"

A moment later the downed man opened one eye. It was royal-blue and ringed with fiery red. Then Ed's mouth fell open. He hiccoughed twice and began to sing a popular television advertising jingle.

"Uh-oh, SpaghettiOs!"

***

That moment changed my life.

Today I live in a rented garage in a trash-littered alley located just off 29th Street. It's been two years since I walked out of Fidelity & Liberty – an event that took place about two hours after Ed O'Donnell went face-first onto the carpet.

I left, that's all.

I dropped out of the middle class... and within a few months, my marriage of six years was *also* kaput.

Call me: The Garage Monk.

These days I sleep on a mattress on the cement floor.

I write a lot of haiku. Yesterday I wrote:

Many green leaves on tree.

But one leaf is blue.

My leaf.

I am very grateful to Ed O'Donnell. When he went face-down on the plastic carpet – after guzzling half a quart of Jameson's during his lunch-break at the Circus Show Bar – I experienced an epiphany that changed my life.

Suddenly, I saw the lies. The Iraq War, and all those breathless announcements from the White House, and the relentless jockeying for position in the offices of Fidelity & Liberty... and my own years of lonely struggle as an English major who had revered the works of Alfred, Lord Tennyson.

Break, break, break,
    On thy cold gray stones, O sea!
        And I would that my tongue could utter
            The thoughts that arise in me.
Break, break, break,
    At the foot of thy crags, O sea!
        But the grace of a day that is dead
           Will never come back to me.

Often at twilight, I sit on the cracked brickwork of my tiny alley porch and mull my destiny. My childhood was a swarm of bitter lies; my marriage to a public relations professional who worked in the downtown Kessler Towers Office Complex had been more of the same.

But I am free of those things now. Today I am free to recite aloud – slowly and thoughtfully – the works of the immortal Alfred, Lord Tennyson.

THE BLOOD OF THE MOSQUITO

Dr. Midnight, our local popular deejay, got killed in his Volkswagen.

I was 14 that summer.

"He tried to dig a hole in the ground with his teeth," said the barber, O.W. Butts. "That's how much pain that old boy was in, after the crash. Like a wounded animal tries to dig a hole with his teeth."

He handed me a green balloon. "You're all done, kid."

I climbed down out of his big iron chair. Some white powder spilled from the side of my head. I gave him the two quarters. I didn't say, "Shut your trap, you shit!" but I wanted to. Dr. Midnight... he'd been my late-night friend on the radio.

"Here they come, the Everly Brothers, with one of their biggest hits."

Never knew what I missed....
        Until I kissed ya!

This was North Florida in the late 1950s, and the air was yellow-thick with lies. Church lies, school lies, family lies – one false move at the dinner table and somebody would fatten your lip for you.

But Dr. Midnight was different. The moon hung at the end of the oak branch outside my window. The Spanish moss rippled in the night breeze. A gleam of light winked against the Chevy parked in the driveway next door. *Never knew what I missed.* And now he was dead. The green Volkswagen had gone head-on into a tree, at better than 60 miles an hour.

The deejay had crawled out of the wreckage. He'd dug at the earth with his teeth. *That's how it is*, I told myself in the darkness. *That's the only real story here.*

***

A couple of weeks after they buried Dr. Midnight, the yearly Tabernacle Revival came to town. They pitched a giant circus tent out at the fairgrounds. Some of us kids rode our bikes out there so we could watch the spectacle from a distance.

They'd ringed the tent with these big yellow lights hooked to a gasoline-powered generator. The air stank of gas and the lights glared, then dimmed, then glared again. A heavy male voice thundered over the loudspeakers: "How many out there will take grace into their hearts? I ask you! How many out there will let yourselves be washed clean in the blood of the Lamb? I ask you!"

The Strangeness

Perched on the seat of my red Schwinn bicycle, I yelled at Shep and Joey: "How do you guys like *that* bullshit?"

They looked uneasy. We were in the ninth grade at Blessed Sacrament School.

"Come on," I hollered at them. "You know it's bullshit – *say* so!" They looked away from me. "You think Dr. Midnight got washed?" I pestered them. "He ate dirt, guys; he tried to eat his way down into the earth. Do you think he got washed at the end, while he was eating dirt?"

They didn't say anything.

I watched the long lines of worshippers moving slowly toward the big red and gold altar at the front of the tent. "If you feel it working in your heart... come on *down*!"

"If you feel the blood of the Lamb alive and breathing deep in your soul... come on *down*!"

I looked down at my left hand: two fat mosquitoes were gorging themselves on the back of it. Splat!

"Here's some blood!" I shouted at Shep and Joey. "Look over here." I waved my wet hand at their frightened faces. "See this blood, boys? Do you see it?

"This here isn't the blood of the Lamb. Nossir, this is the blood of the *mosquito*!"

CRYSTAL RADIO

Midnight. Big yellow moon floats above the black tree branch.

He's sitting in the window.

Touch the wire to the coil... adjust the earplugs until they're snug.

...coming to you live from the downtown studios of WKTT!

Holy smoke! He bought this crystal radio set from a kid named Shep Sawyer. Bought it just this morning. Gave Shep a dollar he'd earned mowing a couple of lawns over on La Hermosa Avenue.

...Elvis gonna do his big hit for you: Hound Dog!

He looks up at the moon. When a piece of rock can put a live voice in your ear, it's easy to believe that a man lives inside that yellow moon.

What the heck *is* everything?

Really, he's half afraid the crystal radio will start talking directly to him.

Hey there, Tommy! How's every little thing? I'm coming to you live from the lunar surface....

(Hello? Hello? This is 1958. This is 1958, talking to 2011. How you doing, 2011? Can you copy, 2011?)

The President, a guy named Ike... he just turned off his bedside lamp. He's got a lot on his mind tonight. Sleep won't come easily, it sure won't. But he needs it. The White House doc keeps telling him –

No matter how hard Tommy Noonan thinks about it, he can't understand how a piece of galena and a wire coil can put a live voice in your ear.

Galena... a little chunk of yellowish rock.

Like that moon, really. Yellowish rock.

What is this power? The way Mr. Jeffries explained it in class... there are waves of electromagnetism. A fancy word, *electromagnetism*, but what the heck does it mean? Apparently, there's a strange form of energy loose in the air... some kind of quivering, flickering light, and that weird light-energy is simply drawn to the stone.

Simply. Just like metal is drawn to a magnet.

Like that guy in the outer-space movie – his eyes lit up, they glowed with a flickering green energy: *whoa*. That guy in the outer-space movie, he'd been invaded by some kind of force contained in a meteorite. That guy in the movie... a farmer, a meteorite crashes into his cornfield, the farmer runs out there, he starts poking at it with a stick. And now the green energy goes creeping up the stick, now it's on the farmer's hands, now it's creeping up his arms: Yikes! It's in his eyes now, they're green, they're glowing, and the farmer starts to babble. He's gurgling like a frog hiding under a rock in the swamp at midnight: Glurk! Glurk!

What the hooey?

It's midnight. Elvis is singing *Hound Dog* in the earplugs. Thanks to the greenish energy trapped deep in the galena. Thanks to the power of the crystal.

Houston, we're right on the money. We're detaching the nose cone in 20 seconds.

Detaching the cone, Eagle, on your mark.

Copy that, Houston. Detaching on our mark.

(Hello? Hello? This is 1958, talking to 1969. Can you copy, 1969? Roger, 1969. Copy that. You're good to go, 1969. You're on the money. Detaching on your mark, 1969.)

"It'll play forever," Shep Sawyer had told his 14-year-old friend Tommy Noonan that morning. "No batteries. No electricity needed. The power's in the crystal."

WHAT WAS THAT?
WAS THAT A GUNSHOT?

Huff got laid off. We downsized, and Huff wound up in the Conference Room. They gave him the envelope with the paycheck for three months and the envelope with the Blue Cross for six months. There were two Wackenhut Security guards in the Conference Room, armed with heavy clubs.

Huff buzzed me on my cell.

"I'm done," he said.

"You're done? Jesus, Larry!"

"Three other guys went down with me. Three guys from Purchasing. There's blood all over the Conference Room."

"Larry, I'm sorry."

"That's okay," he said. "Will you walk me out to my car?"

"Right now? What about... all your stuff?"

"They're going to box everything up. Everything in our desks. They'll box it and send it to us tomorrow, via FedEx."

"Okay. Are you in the lobby?"

"I am."

"I'll be right down."

Larry Huff had given them 15 years of loyal service. He'd worked hundreds of hours of overtime for which he'd never been paid. On at least a dozen occasions, he'd busted ass throughout the weekend so that deadlines would be met.

Now... kaput.

His throat had just been cut.

***

We stood together on Fort Street, beside his green Datsun.

It was a windy afternoon in August, about three o'clock. Above us loomed a china-blue sky, an occasional puffy-white cloud. It was just another afternoon in Palookaville. About twenty yards down the block, the *Polock Johnny's* hot dog guy was packing up his cart.

I looked down at the *Fifth Avenue* candy bar wrapper beside my right shoe....

I shook his hand. "Larry... can I buy you one at Dirty Helen's? Buy you one for the road?"

He studied me for a moment. "Naw," he said. "Thanks, but I better get on home. Cindy... I've got some explaining to do."

Honey... they downsized me.

The Strangeness

I shook his hand a second time. "Call me? If there's anything at all I can do?"

For a moment or two, the hot wind blew his brown hair sideways. Then he climbed into the Datsun. He sat motionless behind the wheel for a few seconds. "Bye," he said. He turned the key and drove off.

A few drops of rain spattered against my face. They were fat drops and strangely warm – and they'd fallen out of a perfectly clear blue sky.

Then the No. 10 bus to Dundalk rumbled into the space Huff had just vacated. The windows were wide open in the heat, and the blue-capped driver was chewing gum. His jaw worked slowly, mechanically.

Pow! I jumped – what was that? Was that a gun? Had a passenger on the bus just fired a weapon? Had he fired a round into the heart of a complete stranger?

No. It was only a backfire.

False alarm.

The old Baltimore City Transit bus farted blue smoke for a couple of seconds... then clattered off into the summer afternoon.

I went back upstairs. I went back to my job.

I never heard from Larry Huff again.

ONE IS NECESSARY,
ONE IS A PIECE OF FATE

Brown's father, dying, struggles to lift his head from the pillow. "You were always a good kid. I love you, Frankie...."

Brown's wiping tears.

Outside the hospital, a windy summer night. The leaves twist, writhe like tortured snakes. Then a quick patter of rain gleams against the black skins of the oaks. We're walking toward the parking lot, Baltimore General.

"Fuck," says Brown. "You know... he worked his guts out at Beth Steel."

"I know, Frank."

"Worked on the Number Two Blast Furnace. Sometimes... more than once – the fucking guy's hair caught fire."

"I hear you."

"I need a drink."

But he sits motionless behind the wheel. The rain trickles along the windshield. This is late July in Crabtown. "You know what he did, Jerry?"

"What's that?"

"A couple of weeks before I started the first grade, he takes me down in the basement. We were living in one of those tiny rowhouses in Dundalk, you know. Argyle Avenue? But we had a little basement. The furnace... he takes me down there one night, he says: 'Okay, you're starting school – so you gotta learn how to fight.' He'd hung a heavy punching bag from a rafter. So he ties the gloves on my hands. They're too big, but he ties 'em on as best he can. He says: 'Okay. Hit the bag.'

"I take a swing. Not much muscle behind it... I'm only six years old. He says, 'Come on, hit it. That's the bully on the school parking lot. Knock his block off, kid!'"

"I take another swing. Still not much there. I'm new at this. He shows me how to throw a punch, a right cross. 'You set him up with your left, Frankie – hook him! Hook him!' He's jabbing the air, trying to show me. Then he comes in with the right cross – the bag jumps: POW!"

Frank sighs. "My pop." He sticks the key in the ignition. "Now he's dying."

What can I say to him?

"He cared about you, Frank."

He nods. "His hair burned, Jerry. That's how hot it was around the Number Two Blast Furnace."

So we drove down to East Baltimore Street, went into the Circus Show Bar. They had some green and purple strobe lights going in there; the lights broke your face up into patches of sliding color. The sound system crackled and spat:

Daddy was a rollin' stone;
  Wherever he laid his hat was his home....

A drum rolled somewhere in the back of the club, but not very loud. "Ladies and gentlemen, say hello to the luscious Kitty Kat!"

A tall blonde stepped onto the tiny stage. She wore silver panties and what looked like two pint-sized fly swatters over her nipples. She moved to the music some, but she seemed pretty listless for the most part. There were only four or five guys in the joint, hunched over their $6 draft beers.

Brown was wiping tears again.

We drank a couple of beers. The next morning Frank learned that his dad had died while we were sitting in the Circus Show Bar. Around one a.m., the doctor said.

I kept thinking of that punching bag, of Frank's tiny six-year-old fists going into the bag. "Come on, slug him! Knock him on his ass, Frankie!"

Crabtown. You ever watched a crab scuttle around the bottom of a bucket? Eyes bulging on their stalks... and that big fighting claw twitching and quivering. That's the real story, isn't it? Isn't that the name of the game? That naked claw... quivering?

MY NAME IS FRANK DEMPSEY

In those days, we lived across the street from the Maryland Penitentiary.

This was 50 years ago, and my old man was dying of cancer. Increasingly frail, and with his eyesight dimming a little more each day, he often sat in his wheelchair on our tiny porch.

I was 15 that summer.

The disease had already destroyed his spine.

But he had some energy left. And whenever he spotted the silhouette looming in the prison window on the other side of Forest Avenue, he'd yell at me:

"Batter up!"

We'd roll his chair into position and he'd lean forward, ready to play catcher. I'd stand in front of him, pretending to swing an imaginary bat.

Once we were ready, the man in the prison window would pretend to wind up. He'd rock backwards and kick one leg high in the air. Then he'd pretend to fire the ball in our direction.

My old man would pretend to catch his fastball, while shouting toward the distant prison wall: "Strike one!"

Day after day, in that summer of 1958, we performed the same ritual. After 10 or 15 "pitches," the man in the barred window would send us a cheerful wave. Then he'd turn away – and we knew we wouldn't see him again until the next morning.

My father died that November.

A few weeks after my high school graduation, and three years after the baseball summer on the porch, we heard a knock at the door.

I remember the moment well. My mother was standing at the kitchen stove, making crab soup. My two younger brothers were off mowing lawns.

I went to the door. Our visitor was a muscular-looking black man who appeared to be in his early 30s. He wore an orange baseball cap: *Orioles*.

"Do you remember me?"

"I'm sorry," I said. "Do I know you?"

"The pitcher!" he said.

His voice broke; for a moment he was crying. "I always told myself: 'No matter how long it takes, when I finally get out of here, I'll stop by that house and I'll thank those two guys.'

"You helped me get through it, man!"

He was shaking my hand, pumping it hard.

"Okay," I said. "I'm glad you made it."

He grinned and doffed the cap. "But why'd you stop?" he said. "I always wondered about that. All of a sudden, right at the end of the summer, you quit sitting on that porch. No more baseball. What happened?"

"Oh," I said. "That was my father in the wheelchair. He had cancer and he died."

His face fell. "I'm sorry."

"It's okay."

"I'm really sorry," he said.

***

About a month after the prisoner was released and paid us that visit, I joined the Navy. I spent 30 years as a shipboard electrician. Several times over those years, I returned to Baltimore. On my last visit in 1998, I drove past the little rowhouse where we'd played baseball with the man in the window.

The house was still there, but the prison had been torn down. The State of Maryland had built a new maximum-security facility way out in northern Baltimore County.

Everything changes. Everything ends. But I've never forgotten the summer of '58, or the man who stood in the prison window and pretended to pitch.

My name is Frank Dempsey.

I died in 2008.

THE ALIENS HAVE LANDED

The telephone rang. Magoon picked it up. A panicked voice crackled in his ear. "Are you a reporter?"

"I try to be," said Magoon. "What's up, sir?"

"Is this the newsroom of the *Evening Sun*?"

"Absolutely."

"This is Clint Wysocki, over in South Baltimore. You'll say I'm nuts – but an alien spacecraft just landed in my backyard."

"You're nuts," said Magoon. Then: "Hah-hah. Just kidding, Mr. Wysocki."

"I don't have time for your shenanigans, fella. What's your name?"

"Magoon."

"Get down here, Magoon. I'm at 2211 Butner Way. It's off Light Street. I'm looking at the spaceship even as we speak. I've got the binoculars on it. This will go front page, worldwide."

"What's it look like?"

"The spaceship?"

"Correct."

"Like an aluminum cigar the length of a football field."

"Thank you," said Magoon. "Can you hang on a sec?"

"Ten-four, Magoon."

Magoon cupped the mouthpiece with one hand, then bellowed in the direction of the city desk. "Hey, I got a bozo on Line Two, says an alien spaceship just landed in his backyard."

Honeycutt, the assistant city editor, didn't hesitate. "You on deadline, Magoon?"

"Nope."

"Where is he?"

"South Baltimore."

"Okay," said Honeycutt. "He's only a few minutes away. Take one of the staff cars and check it out. He's probably a lunatic... but you never know."

"Right," said Magoon. "Will do." He un-cupped the mouthpiece.

"I'm on my way, Mr. Wysocki. See you in ten."

"You better hurry," said Wysocki. "The spaceship is jiggling. It's lit up. Any minute, the aliens will start pouring out."

***

Magoon drove south on Light Street.

I want vodka, he told himself. Everything has become so goddam hard, without Dorinda.

The Strangeness

Really, all he wanted was to sit in a steaming-hot tub, moaning softly and taking huge gulps of icy vodka.

That's the price of love, he told himself.

***

Wysocki turned out to be a senile octogenarian with monster-bad halitosis.

"Here!" he shouted at Magoon as Magoon stepped out of the Evening Sun staff car. "Look through these!"

He handed the reporter a pair of huge, heavy binoculars. "Point these babies at that garage roof over there. The green garage roof across the street. Do you see it?"

"I do."

"Eyeball that roof, Magoon."

He did. But all he saw was... green shingles.

"I'm not picking up a spaceship, Mr. Wysocki."

The old man's face began tightening up, as if screws were being turned behind it. His eyes shrank until they were mere dagger-points. "You aren't *looking* right, Magoon. Gimme the goddam things!"

Magoon handed them over. The old man struggled with the focusing wheel... cursed... then barked: "Got it! Aluminum cigar! Get over here!"

He was holding them in place now. They were focused and ready to go. Magoon eased in beside him, then fitted his eyes into the eye-cups on the cumbersome German-made device.

"See it?"

Magoon swiveled his eyeballs, searching.

"Do you see the goddam spaceship or don't you?"

Magoon struggled. "Mr. Wysocki," he said, "I don't think –"

But then he spotted something. For a moment, it *did* look like a huge aluminum cigar. But it wasn't. It was a metal clothesline, that's all. The simple truth was that the old man had turned the magnification on the binoculars all the way up to the max – which made the glittering metal clothesline look like a giant metal cylinder. On the binocular lenses – but *only* there – the metal wire did resemble an immense, hovering spaceship.

"It's a clothesline, Mr. Wysocki."

"What? What? A clothesline?"

"It's your neighbor's clothesline. You've got the magnification set too high." He handed the binoculars back to their owner.

"What?" snarled Wysocki. "What's your game, buster?" The old man's mouth looked like a red wound. Inside that wound, his yellow teeth were jagged-scary. Had he been filing them down – sharpening them in some dimly lit basement workshop?

"You're a bullshit artist, Magoon."

Magoon was already walking back toward the staff car. "I'm sorry, Mr. Wysocki."

The old man ran after the staff car. He chased it for more than half a block, while screaming and leaping. "You're a bullshit artist, do you hear me? Go jump in the Chesapeake Bay, you bullshit artist!"

Magoon drove slowly past Ft. McHenry, the birthplace of the Star-Spangled Banner.

Vodka, he told himself with a weary sigh. *Nothing else can help me now.*

WAITING FOR THE CALL

Epp sat in his cubicle drinking a cup of Awake and waiting for the call.

He looked down: his fingers were quivering a little.

He noticed a spot of yellow sunshine glowing against the dull brown carpet. About the size of a dime. The sun was an immense ball of flaming gases, nine million miles distant, and the bright spot consisted of trillions of photons that had been generated within its nuclear furnace.

Epp knew these facts. They were objectively true, but difficult to believe. Sunlight. How strange it seemed. He remembered a comment by Edward Hopper, the American artist: "All I wanted was to paint the drama of sunlight on a wall."

The phone rang, and he sat up straight. Was this it?

"Got your coffee?" asked a bright voice on the other end. It was only Green, the District Manager. "Sales meeting in five minutes," said Green. "Conference Room B."

"Okay," said Epp.

Maybe they'd tell him at the meeting?

No... everyone else had been told on the phone. They'd all gotten calls from Bronson. "Hi, Carl. This is Skip Bronson, up in Schenectady? I'm afraid I have some bad news."

Look at me, Epp told himself. I'm sick with fear.

What would a real man do? That was easy: a real man would lock and load. He'd fight back. He'd wander the halls at Corporate, picking off the execs one by one.

Epp took a sip of his Awake.

Three days before, he'd driven around a crushed squirrel on I-28. The creature had been reduced to a lump of mangled red meat, and nothing more. That was the reality. And the sun... the sun was a nuclear reactor, that's all. A monster furnace floating in space. And the people in his office... they were like ants creeping back and forth across the sand, hunting food. Hunting red meat from a mangled squirrel.

The phone rang. He sat up straight in his swivel-chair. But it was only Marge calling from home. "Hon," she said. "Don't forget, we've got Lindsay's Honor Assembly tonight. It's at six-thirty in the Main Auditorium."

"I'm on it," said Epp. "No problem."

"Any news yet?"

"Nothing," said Epp. "I guess they're gonna wait until after the sales meeting."

"Maybe they won't call you."

"No," said Epp. "They'll call. You know the score, Marge. It's a done deal. Sales were down 30 percent last quarter, and I'm near the bottom of the totem pole."

She sighed. "Okay. Good luck, hon."

He hung up. Took a last sip of his Awake. Rose to his feet. For a fleeting moment, he remembered his father sitting in the wheelchair at Westminster Acres. Scowling. "You didn't get here in time – now it's too late for ice cream!"

"Sorry, dad. Traffic backup... an accident on I-28."

"I wanted ice cream!"

He put his hand on the door of the cubicle, and the phone rang.

He was due at the sales meeting... should he pick it up or let it go?

He grabbed it. "Good morning. Epp here."

Silence for a moment. The little dime-sized spot of sunlight had vanished from the carpet. Then a voice said: "This is Skip Bronson, up in Schenectady."

"Hey, Skip. How you doing?"

"Going good, thanks. But I'm afraid I have some bad news."

EVERYTHING HERE EATS SOMETHING ELSE

More than anything else in the world, Mooney feared religion, because he knew religion could make him crazy. *Dear God*, Mooney often prayed, *I'm asking you respectfully and sincerely: Please leave me alone!*

But God apparently had other ideas.

On Saturday, the ninth of January, Mooney found himself looking directly into the yellow eye of a Great Lakes seagull. This happened on the parking lot of the Big KMart. The bird was in the middle of beak-stabbing a hunk of discarded Burger King, and Mooney saw how his dagger-sharp claws were digging into the filthy ice that lay along the edge of the curb.

That was bad enough – the way the gull's bone-spurs were splintering bits of ice as the gull fought to *eat, eat*, and the way the crystal bits were kicking up beside the blackened sidewalk. But then things got even stranger... as Mooney met the creature's yellow-glaring eye.

Whoa, Mooney told himself. *Help!*

He could feel the weirdness, the pure blue craziness pulling at his chin. What *was* that gull's eye, anyway? A yellow pellet floating in the clear liquid of a bone socket and no larger than a pea... and yet that pellet was wired with half a million spidery nerve lines carrying electrochemical impulses from the eye straight on up to the bird's chattering, flickering brain!

"Calm down," Mooney told himself. "It's just another Saturday afternoon in Palookaville – what is there to fear?"

It was true. The town of Palookaville beneath the winter twilight: what could be more familiar-looking? What could be safer? This was his native burg, wasn't it? The streetlights were already on; they glowed softly in the settling dusk. And Mooney could smell the aroma of freshly baked bread – more familiar comfort. And that corner gas station... that huge golden Shell looming against the winter sky –

Yes, this town was comfortable. It soothed. (Provided you didn't look too closely – because things could *change,* up close.)

Mooney had seen it happen, more than once.

That seagull's eye could balloon way up on you – could become a pulsing bag of green-streaked reptiles fighting to get out. Or a black spider might suddenly appear on the white-painted roof of the Big KMart, a spider the size of Winnebago, and *then* what? Most of the time, Mooney kept his eyes focused on the ground. He had learned that if he kept his gaze locked on the grass or the cement, the strangeness could be held at bay. All that remained then was to shut his mind down... which he could usually accomplish by simply repeating a mindless TV jingle over and over again.

Uh-oh, Spaghetti-O!
Uh-oh, Spaghetti-O!

"I'll be fine," Mooney often told himself as he strolled through Palookaville with his eyes on the ground. "I won't be going back to the Locked Ward, not ever!"

But he couldn't shut out everything. Once in a while, in spite of his best efforts, a vision would creep in. How well he remembered that dreadful night, two winters before, when he'd witnessed a truly strange event – the chewing of a piece of beef by an elderly woman who sat in the window of the Ponderosa Steak House.

It was night, January, ten below zero: the moon hung like a lump of gleaming ice in the violet-tinged blackness of the winter sky. And then Tom Mooney made a terrible mistake. Trudging across the packed snow that fronted the Ponderosa's Main Dining Room, he looked up just in time to see the old lady sliding a hunk of bloody cow into her distended yap.

A moment later, the two of them were staring at each other.

Stricken with horror, Mooney stood paralyzed on his side of the glass. Helpless, he watched the octogenarian struggle to crush and tear the cow flesh into fragments small enough to be swallowed.

Her eyes were bulging... like the eyes of a crab will bulge if you poke at them with a stick – *she was fighting to ingest that cow meat!*

Staggered by the sight of her laboring jaw, where eight different muscles were straining to the max, Mooney was suddenly confronting a terrifying truth: *Everything here eats something else.*

Ears ringing with fear, he stumbled away from the illuminated window and nearly went down in the snow. It was all too true: *Everything here eats something else.*

And who could save him now... now that he'd seen the stark reality up close?

"Dear Lord," he prayed fervently, again and again. "Please... please... won't you let me *be*?"

OUR INVISIBLE WORLD

This morning around ten-fifteen, I told Dr. Horn that I no longer know what anything is. That's how I expressed it. I said: "Dr. Horn, if you want the truth, I don't know what anything is."

He looked at me for a few seconds. Then he scribbled something on his yellow legal pad. "That's interesting," he said. "Can you elaborate?"

"All right," I said. "Wall Street has melted down. Am I correct?"

"Well …"

"The economy is in the toilet, and the planet is heating up. The Wall Street vampires are drinking our blood. Yesterday we lost a piece of ice the size of Connecticut. The goddam thing fell off the Arctic Rim, or whatever. The oceans are rising; we could lose Hong Kong any day. Plus, I feel a new weirdness in my spine. My vertebrae aren't meshing properly. Yesterday, without meaning to, I suddenly hopped. I was walking down Jefferson Street, an ordinary morning, and all at once I hopped. It was involuntary, I assure you. And there's more. When I turn on the TV these days, I have trouble knowing what they mean. Oh, and I read in USA Today that human beings are actually on fire. Like, when you eat a sandwich – bologna, lettuce, pickle, a little mustard – what actually happens is, you ignite that sandwich. Huh? There's no flame, as such... but way down there at the molecular level, oxidation is the order of the day. And that's fire. Oxidation is simply fire. Remember tenth-grade chemistry lab? Oxidation. Anyway, I also read that we're swarming with bacteria. We think we're pretty elevated creatures... you know, homo erectus and all that. But the fact is that we're actually carrying ten times as many bacterial cells as human cells. We're bacteria dumps, Dr. Horn. We're absolutely groaning under the load. And that's pretty humbling, don't you think? We're laboring under these enormous continents of leaky bacterial slush – goddamit, they've got us hauling them around town all day! I'm exhausted just thinking about it, and then I saw this plastic model of a human spine – it's just a series of hinged plates, you bend over and the plates all readjust like something on an automated assembly line, and you ask yourself: What really happens when I brush my teeth? If you slosh some mouthwash around in there, do entire cities of bacteria start screaming and dying? Or would it be better not to think about the bacteria sneaking along your gum line? You see, it's pretty damn strange... the way we're told that most of our world is invisible. Huh? Huh? It's invisible, and the atoms and the various quarks, the top quarks and the bottom quarks, the bosons and the muons – they're all invisible. And then the molecules keep jiggering through the Brownian motion – did you have the Brownian motion in the tenth grade? Here are the molecules, they're all quivering and twitching and whatnot, and that's the Brownian motion. Am I making any sense at all, Dr. Horn?"

Dr. Horn looked at me for a few seconds. Then he scribbled something on his yellow pad. He said: "Do you feel anxious, Mr. Doyle?"

I nodded. "I do."

"Can you elaborate?"

"Okay," I told him. "I hope I can get this across. It's like... in our invisible world, nothing has any time for itself. Okay? Like, I watched this chipmunk the other day. Just a little guy. He ran up the side of the bird-feeder, and he looked inside. Then he darted inside. He was eating the birdseed – I saw a few husks go flying. But then he darted back outside and took a look around. Huh? He took a look... then he zipped back inside. Husks flying. Huh?

"So I asked myself: What's going on here? And after a while, I figured it out. He was eating birdseed... but he was also afraid of being eaten. Any minute, a red-tailed hawk could drop out of the sky, nail his tiny ass, devour him in a New York minute. So he couldn't eat for long. See what I mean? Quick little bites... husks flying. He had no time for himself, no time at all. I watched him darting in and out of the bird-feeder, and I thought: If only I could send that little guy on a Bahamas cruise!"

"I see," said Dr. Horn. He scribbled something on his yellow pad. Then he said: "I'm sorry, but I think our time is up. Please pay the cashier on the way out."

THE SINGING FISH

They'd been fighting all afternoon – and now they were fighting over Miro's "The Singing Fish."

"Miro is all about triangles," said Maloney. "I can tell you one thing for sure: that painting has nothing to do with a fish."

Honey Lee Harris glared at him. "Thanks, Mr. In-the-Know Critic. You're so full of shit, it's unbelievable!"

Her voice rose like a siren on "unbelievable," and the blue-uniformed security guard took a step toward them. "No loud talking in the gallery," he crooned softly in their direction. "Please remember: this is the Chicago Museum of Contemporary Art."

"Sorry," whispered Maloney. "We forgot ourselves."

"He's impossible," hissed Honey Lee.

"That's okay," said the guard. "But if you two have an issue, why not take it on down to the Museum Café? It's on Level B."

"Thank you," they both said.

***

They bought Mango Mango Green Teas and sat at a glass table. It was Wednesday afternoon in Chicago. Nothing really tragic was occurring here. These were just two young people who frequently irritated the shit out of each other.

"I don't see why you keep getting your back up," said Maloney. "I'm an *art* student, Honey Lee. What did you expect?"

"Yeah, well, I paid the entire goddam utility bill last month," said Honey Lee.

Maloney groaned. "What's that got to do with Miro's triangles? I told you I'd get a job as soon as the semester ends."

She snickered. "Yeah, right."

He took a sip of Mango Mango Green Tea. "Sweetheart, all I was saying... if you think about it, a Miro fish is nothing more than a series of triangles linked together in an abstract design. Here… let me show you."

A moment later he was drawing on his napkin with a PaperMate Flair.

"See what I mean?" he said as he slid the napkin toward her.

The Strangeness

Back upstairs, in Gallery No. 47, the blue-uniformed security guard had moved in closer to The Singing Fish.

"Isn't it amazing," said the guard in a low undertone, so that no one else could hear, "the endless variety of human types who wander through this gallery each day?"

The Singing Fish didn't reply for a moment. Then his left eye – his staring, cobalt-blue eye, which was really nothing more than a brightly painted circle – opened and closed in a good-natured wink.

AMONG THE JELLIES

Halloran was smart. *Too* smart. And it was killing him. Being smart had ruined Halloran's life. Now he yearned for one thing and one thing only: to be dumber.

"If I could just be really stupid," Halloran told himself each morning as he sipped his Maxwell House. "Wouldn't that be wonderful? To taste the joys of being dull-witted... maybe even insensate! How I'd love to be an unconscious boulder deep in the Rockies, or perhaps a cardboard deer."

Halloran couldn't forget the last thing Dorinda had said to him, as she lugged her tanning lamp out to the Volkswagen Golf: "You may be smarter than I am, Halloran, but that doesn't mean I have to tolerate your shit!"

"Tolerate?" Halloran had wailed at her departing figure. "*Tolerate*? Hon, I gave you every goddam thing you *wanted*!"

But it was too late. The VW Golf had clattered around the corner, and poor Halloran had spent the next week sitting in the empty breakfast nook eating *Cheeto Puffs* from a jumbo-sized cellophane bag and washing them down with gallons of malt liquor.

He was suffering immensely. Fortunately, however, the South Marshfield Community College was on its week-long spring break, so he was spared the anguish of talking about relative clauses and grading dozens of "Process Essays" each day. But the week was speeding by, and Halloran felt pretty much like a decaying turd. His stomach had gone sour on him, and his midriff had ballooned way up on the *Cheetos*.

"I've got to get out of this apartment," he told himself. "It's haunted with the memory of Dorinda."

What Halloran needed was a neutral setting, an anonymous space where he could sit and stare straight ahead... and maybe even drool a little. He needed a place where he could practice being *dumb*.

As good fortune would have it, the mailman soon came to his rescue – by dropping a colorful flier through the slot in his front door.

The Chicago Aquarium invites you...
To visit the mysterious world of the JELLIES!

Blinking slowly and burping malt, Halloran read about the "Major Jellyfish Exhibition" that was about to open at the lakefront fish palace.

Fascinating and intriguing, jellyfish are millions of years older than even the oldest dinosaurs....

Halloran rapped the flier with the backs of his knuckles. "That's it," he told himself. "I'm going."

Jellyfish couldn't swim, according to the flier. Hell, they couldn't even see where they were going – since they didn't have eyes. All they knew how to do was *pulse*... while drifting helplessly wherever the current wanted to take them.

They're really dumb, thought Halloran. *I can learn from them.*

Two hours later, he was standing in front of a pulsing "Blue Blubber"** – a really strange-looking animal outfitted with eight jelly arms that waved in every direction at once. The Blue Blubber wasn't just weird... it was *super*-weird, since each one of the waving arms was equipped with its own tiny mouth.

So... the arm grabs a passing fish, stings it into submission, and then the mouth on that particular arm starts eating the fish?

Whoa, thought Halloran.

Yet he felt strangely peaceful here. He felt calmed, soothed.

A moment later he was watching an aquarium attendant push a big sweeper-broom along the corridor that flanked the Blue Blubber's tank.

The broom-man wore a brass name plate above the pocket of his work shirt: *Mr. Lincoln.*

Halloran felt a surge of jagged excitement. He stepped toward the man. "Mr. Lincoln?"

"Uh-huh," said Mr. Lincoln. "All right now. What's up?"

All at once, Halloran's eyes were swimming with tears. "Do you think... I mean...is there any chance I could *work* here?"

The janitor thought for a moment. "You want to work in maintenance?"

"I do," said Halloran. "I really do."

"Well," said Mr. Lincoln. "That's quaint. Tell you what: I'll run you down to the Aquarium Office and we'll get you started with an application. How would that be?"

**The Jelly Blubber (*Catostylus mosaicus*), also known as the *Blue Blubber Jellyfish*, is the most commonly encountered jellyfish along the Australian eastern coast and large swarms sometimes appear in estuarine waters.

–Wikipedia

STRANGENESS

Have you ever been hit by the strangeness?

I mean... have you ever noticed the very large amount of weirdness out there?

I remember, back in 1986, I took a long hard look at a toco toucan in the Baltimore Zoo and everything changed for me. If you've ever scrutinized the toco, you'll know what I'm talking about. He's got this enormous bill the color of a wet orange popsicle and his eyes are like two ice-blue M&Ms pasted on the top. Those eyes follow you everywhere – while the toco keeps up a steady barrage of "throat-croaks" and "bill-clacks."

"Clack-*clack*... clack-*clack*!"

I looked at the toco and I asked myself: "Who put the *dih* in the *dih*-dih-dih?"

Q. How did life come about? Did sunlight ripple across a swamp puddle 1.5 billion years ago, triggering some major activity deep within the bubbling glop?

(Vonnegut: "Some mud sat up – it's that simple.")

(Okay, fine, Kurt... but *why* did that mud sit up? Vonnegut was curiously silent on *that* issue, don't you think?)

***

Anyway, I was walking along 29th Street one afternoon about 20 years ago, when I suddenly spotted *strangeness*. I spotted a junked-out car sitting in the middle of a vacant lot. It was a big old green Mercury with the windshield smashed out, just baking in the July heat.

And there was a very large woman resting on the backseat.

She looked me straight in the eye... and her eye held *my* eye... and I damn near crapped myself. *That can't be a woman on that backseat*, I muttered inwardly, *it's too goddam hot out here*.

But it was. It was a woman, a glaring woman, and she was not happy with me.

Strangeness! She tried to pull me toward her. Truly. She controlled this super-powerful magnetic field... and for a few moments I could feel the energy of it working on my face. Trust me here: my cheeks and the slack flesh under my chin – they were pulling away from me, they wanted to go to her, to *be* with her, to live with her forever in her auto darkness, to swelter with her in the back of that junked-out car.

In that instant, I knew her forever: *the woman in the back of the car*.

Creepy? Please believe me: there's more than enough creepiness to go around.

In those days, of course, I was living in the abandoned garage off 29th Street. I was also drinking a fair amount of *Wildcat* malt liquor. Why should I pretend about that? And there's more: on a couple of truly terrifying occasions, I woke up at 3 a.m. to find several women in black robes stacking firewood against my window. One look and I understood the worst: the goddam alley was full of witches, and they were getting ready to burn me out!

Suddenly, it was life or death. I threw open the door of the garage and lunged at them with a big yard-rake, I'LL KILL YOU BITCHES, and they scattered, and as they ran they turned into overhanging tree branches, into a stop sign, into a parked car, into a black cat that fled from my rake, screaming with rage –

I never saw the car-woman again, of course. But I don't *need* to see her again – she lives inside me now, glaring and scowling and forever enraged, and the darkness flows like smoke from her pitiless gaze....

Q. Ever looked into the glinting depths of a cat's eye?

Strangeness. There's a Man-in-the-Moon, please take my word for it, and one night you're walking and it's late… and you're looking at that knobby jaw of his, that bad-boy grin of his, those sardonic eyes –

And bingo! – they're quick-as-a-blink transported from the moon to the cabbie's face, as the cab pulls up beside you on 29th Street and now the Man-in-the-Moon leans out the window of his taxi, and he chuckles deep in his sardonic throat:

Want a lift, pal?

FAMILY TROUBLE

Riley's grandmother, Bridget, dead 50 years, took a long pull at the blackened stump of her Hav-a-Tampa. The lit end glowed cherry-red.

"Boyo, I hate to tell you," she growled at the dumbfounded Riley, who'd nearly toppled from his stool at the Emerald Isle, "but yer a major fookin' disappointment, all around."

Riley blinked back at her. What could this uncanny visitation mean? "Grandma Bridget," he said to the apparition with the smoldering stogy jutting from its scowling mug, "I don't get it. This can't be happening. You passed way back in the late 1960s... and yet here you are again! The way you handle that cigar – I'd recognize it anywhere."

She glared at him. "Get off your arse," she snapped. "Follow me."

He did.

The barkeep, Mulcahy, looked up from the sports page of the Baltimore *Evening Sun*. "What's this?" said Mulcahy. "You ain't closing the joint tonight?"

***

Outside, on Waterfront Street, the stunned Riley clung to a lamp pole. "Grandma," he stammered. "This can't be an actual event. This, like, totally flies in the face of science."

She barked with sudden laughter. "Do ya know what science is, boyo?"

"No. What is it?"

"Cat piffle," said Grandma Bridget. "All these bosons and muons and quarks they've been feedin' you of late – can't you see they're tryin' to eat your brain?"

Riley blinked harder.

"In my day," said Grandma Bridget, "we didn't need the muons and the bosons. We had something much better. We had *poteen*."

Riley's mouth was hanging open by now. He looked like a thoroughly drugged sheep. "Poteen?" he finally managed to croak at her.

"Tater mash in a glass jar," glowered Bridget. "And the still looked just like an outhouse – we fooled the fookin' Tans every single time."

"The Tans?" said Riley.

"My God," said Bridget. "You don't even know the fookin' *Tans*?"

The Strangeness

"I'm sorry," said Riley. "I'm just... I've been... none of this... I'm just an English instructor, Grandma Bridget!"

Her green eyes widened with horror. "English? Yer teachin' *English*? Jesus, Mary and Joseph!" Now she crossed herself hurriedly, and the Hav-a-Tampa threw a plume of wavy smoke.

"Hey, it's a living," wailed the community college instructor. "Come on, Grammaw... everybody has to make a buck!"

"Sheeeeeeeett!" said Grandma Bridget.

"I've got child-support," said Riley. "Things have been... difficult. My second marriage..."

He trailed off. She was sneering openly now. "Yer *second* marriage? Yer only supposed to marry *once*, you weak toad!"

Riley was flapping one hand at her now, trying to drive the cigar smoke off. "I know. I know. But things happened. I won't lie, Grandma – Dorinda gave me the boot. I'm living in an abandoned garage. Yesterday... please trust me on this: yesterday, a BG&E meter reader on my street was transformed into a fire-snorting bull!"

"What? *What*?" Her jaw was sticking way out now. "A bull, you say – and he was breathin' fookin' *fire*?"

"That's it. Honest."

She thought for a moment, then leaned in closer to her grandson. He smelled something sweet, something cloying, with an undertone of rotted tater. *Poteen*.

"Listen to me," said Grandma Bridget. "Nothing's the way it looks. Got it?"

"Okay," said Riley. "But –"

"*Got* it? Nothin's the way it looks, and they're doin' their best to eat your fookin' brain. Can you repeat after me?"

"Huh?"

"Can you repeat after me? Repeat this: Dorinda, kiss my royal Irish ass! Say it."

"Grandma, I feel silly."

"*Do* it!"

"Dorinda… kiss my royal Irish ass!"

She nodded. For a moment, she even smiled. Then her features collapsed and her eyes shrank way down to glinting b-b's. "Stay strong, boyo – and don't take any *sheeeett* from the Tans!"

A moment later, with a loud hissing sound, she was drawn into the overhanging street lamp.

Like a puff of smoke sucked into a powerful vacuum cleaner, Grandma Bridget had vanished without a trace!

Back inside the Emerald Isle, Riley ordered a double on the rocks. His palsied hand shook as he lifted it toward his mouth.

"What's the deal?" said Mulcahy. "You're white as a sheet."

Riley nodded. "Family trouble," he said.

ENCOUNTER WITH
A FIRE-SNORTING BULL

In the debris-strewn wake of his second marriage, Riley moved into an abandoned garage on 29th Street and began to lose his sanity.

It felt that way, anyhow.

What else could Riley conclude – after watching a brown-uniformed Baltimore Gas & Electric Company meter reader turn into a fire-snorting bull?

It happened on a Wednesday afternoon in July, around five o'clock.

Riley was sitting at the one piece of furniture he'd managed to salvage from his second divorce... a white-plastic Big KMart SleekLine Patio Table marred by a yellow-brown cigarette burn, right in the middle.

There was also a single white-plastic chair.

Riley sat on that chair drinking quart bottles of a low-end malt liquor... *Wildcat*.

In order to pay his $65-a-month rent and his child support, Riley was teaching "Grunt English" – three sections of English 101, aka "Intro to Basic Composition" – out at the Baltimore County Community College. Three days a week, he rode the No. 10 Bus out to campus and told them about gerunds and split infinitives. Then he took the bus back to the garage.

But Riley was off today.

He was pouring the *Wildcat* into a plastic *Burger King* cup that had been left behind by the garage's previous tenant.

Riley was in a lot of pain. For a while, he'd been playing his $6.99 Chinese radio... but then he'd suddenly found himself listening to a "Golden Oldie": *Never knew what I missed... until I kissed ya!*

Riley had blubbered. He'd wept like a heartbroken lake loon on the darkest night of the year. He'd pounded the white-plastic SleekLine with his fists.

"Why do men live?" he'd asked himself again and again.

But no answers had been forthcoming.

Now he sat, numb with spent sorrow, before his rapidly dwindling supply of *Wildcat*. Riley had only 40 cents until payday – still four days off. He also had 124 "Persuasion Essays" to grade before the next morning.

Bummerino.

How had he sunk to these depths? A Grunt English teacher with no car, no healthcare coverage and no Individual Retirement Account! And what was his future, really? *I'll end up in a rented room*, he told himself. *I'll be one of those graying, slowly fading losers with a dry cough and pee stains on his underwear....*

How could Dorinda have done this to him?

Sighing, he lifted the *Burger King* cup... but then froze as a strange, singsong-like voice suddenly caught his ear.

"Gas man! Gas man! BG&E... gas man!"

Still holding the BK cup, Riley staggered over to the sagging garage door. With a grunt of effort – the goddam *wood* was warped! – he forced that door open.

All at once, Riley was looking into the bulging, sky-blue eyes of a Baltimore Gas & Electric Company meter reader.

"Ho," he croaked at the utility operative. Then, in a desperate bid to break the ensuing, truly weird silence: "How you been getting *by*?"

It was a profoundly arresting moment.

Startled by the suddenly opening door, the meter reader had frozen in his tracks.

Now a deep shudder went rippling over his thick, glaring features.

Amazed, Riley watched those features begin to swell. His nose... that blunt organ was ballooning now, was already grotesquely distended, so that the man's nostrils were huge tunnels of black darkness... from which scarlet flames jetted, throwing boiling smoke!

"Holy..." said Riley.

He wasn't looking at a brown-uniformed meter reader anymore – now he was eyeball to eyeball with a sacred, fire-snorting bull!

Suddenly, he felt better. *I think I'm gonna make it*, Riley told himself while the great-hoofed Taurus pawed angrily at the asphalt outside his door. *I think I'm gonna be okay!*

SISYPHUS LOVES THE ROCK

Goddam price of gasoline –

And I've got this spastic colon-thing going, these blue pills I take? The blue chemical "tricks" the gut muscles into relaxing for a few minutes. I blame Father Horstnagel. Down on the molecular level, it would be nice to know what's happening –

Ever looked closely at a Walking Stick? Horrifying! I mean, the goddam thing is alive, okay? Knobby-headed, and a tiny pair of emerald-hued eyes hanging off the stick? One eye hanging off each side of the stick? You'd swear you were looking at a stick, and then the fucking thing moves on you, and you realize: "That's no stick – that's a Walking Stick! That's an insect programmed to look like a stick!" –

Father Horstnagel wore a black gown, I'm sure it had a name. He also wore a dorky little three-cornered hat: the biretta. He hopped around town, collecting money under various pretexts.

Scary? Hey, the woods are full of weirdness. Everywhere you look, it's so strange you want to dial 911. Call in the Marines! And then I pick up the USA Today – what do I find? All these toads are exploding in Belgian ponds. This is no joking matter. Thousands of brown-spotted toads, and they're spontaneously inflating in Belgium, some sort of inner gaseous event, ka-plooey, toad guts in your face. I totally blame Father Horstnagel, not just for World War I, but also for the general kinkiness, the fruitcake episodes, nobody has a clue, with entire Chinese empires collapsing, toads detonating in every direction, and what do they tell us by way of explanation? "It's a flaw in the DNA." All right. Ask yourself: Does that satisfy you? Does "a flaw in the DNA" satisfy you? I mean, is it all electrical, or what? These molecules – I assume we're talking about electrons zipping in and out of different holding patterns? Forming ions, and what not? And that causes the violence? The insane killing everywhere – and the soft yellow moon on a summer night? Is there an architect's rendering we can eyeball, maybe?

Before he came hopping into our town, Father Horstnagel had been a U.S. Army chaplain in the Pacific. He'd blessed men on ships, men who were about to ride the landing boats onto Japanese-held islands. While they died, Father Horstnagel went down to the Captain's table and ate the flapjacks with the Aunt Jemima Molasses. God hovered in the ventilation shaft, only four feet from the priest's bobbing head. Father Horstnagel's large yellow teeth sank into the flapjacks. Good syrup. Sweet, but a tart aftertaste. Full-bodied. Good syrup. The first shells landed among the boats, ripping through the young boys in the steel helmets.

It's not clear how the hominids evolved down through the Holocene to finally culminate in Father Horstnagel. But they got there. All those Precious Blood Fathers – a pack of starved Germans – all those lean guys with the fearsome body odor. Wild, wild, how the hominids somehow evolved all the way to the priest in the black gown and the funny hat. Don't ask me to unravel it. You'll start my spastic colon going again.

I STARTED BREATHING VERY FAST, IN THE CAR

A car door slamming...

You don't know me – you don't inhabit my timeframe. This is 1967, here on this page, and I just got out of the car.

Now I'm standing in a phone booth in the northern Virginia suburb of Falls Church and I'm talking to a psychiatrist.

"Is this an emergency, Mr. Quayle?"

"No, sir. No, Dr. Zentner, it's not."

"Zenton."

"No, Dr. Zenton. It's not. I'm just... well, I started breathing very fast, in the car? Gasping, almost. And things looked... strange. A weird... and now everything seems shiny. And I tasted metal in my mouth. I tasted it. I got your number from this guy in my insurance office."

"Uh-huh."

"I told him – he's a salesman, too? We're at Liberty and Fidelity inWashington? I told him I might be nuts."

"I see. You're an insurance man?"

"Yes. Well... *trying*. Hah-hah!"

"Trying?"

"I'm new. Signed on at Liberty and Fidelity only four months ago. But I've already completed their training course. I'm off and running! Making cold calls now, making 'em every day – hah-hah!"

"All right. But why are you laughing?"

"Laughing? Am I? See... what happened, I was driving down Lee Highway, headed off to my cold calls, and then everything got very strange. True weirdness crept in. The other cars all looked very shiny, and all at once everything seemed pointless. And I'm a college graduate, hah-hah."

"What college?"

"University of Maryland– the Cow College. That's what I named it – the Cow College! Anyway, I started gasping and I couldn't seem to get enough oxygen. Then I got woozy. I got terribly woozy, so I pulled off the road and I got on this pay phone, *voila*! I had your number in my shirt pocket. My friend said you helped him – Bill Brown. You know Bill Brown, Liberty and Fidelity?"

"I do know Mr. Brown."

"I was gasping. I thought I might pass out."

"Uh-huh."

"I got your number from Bill Brown."

"All right, Mr. Quayle. Where are you right now?"

"I'm at a Burger King. Falls Church Burger King. I know you can't speculate, Dr. Zentner, but do think I might be mentally ill?"

"Zenton. I think you're probably having an anxiety attack, Mr. Quayle."

"You do?"

"I do. Here's my suggestion: go into that Burger King and get yourself a paper bag and then breathe into that paper bag 20 times. In and out, 20 times. That will restore the CO_2 in your system. You've been hyperventilating, Mr. Quayle."

"I have?"

"That gasping? That's hyperventilation, that's what that is. Breathe into your bag 20 times and call my office Monday and make an appointment with my secretary, Mrs. French."

"Okay, will do. Will do. Mrs. French."

"Good luck, Mr. Quayle."

***

This is all happening way back in 1967, so the only way to experience it now is to read this page.

My hair is light brown, back then. I weigh 40 pounds less.

I'm exhaling into the Burger King bag. Oxygen out… CO_2 in.

Oxygen out… CO_2 in.

I'm all right. I'm all right. But now I pause for a moment to study the daffy-looking cartoon of the Burger King. He's painted right on the side of the bag.

Big gold crown...

He's a strange-looking dude, that Burger King. I mean, what kind of a world am I in, a king with a golden crown on a bag? And he's inflating... he's shrinking with every breath I take.

Oxygen out... CO_2 in.

I'm 27. That's factual. Forty years from now, I'll write a story about the day I called Dr. Z from a pay phone in northern Virginia. That's what I tell myself: *At 67, I'll write about 27*!

I'm gonna be fine.

Yes, indeedy. I'm sitting in the car. It's 1967. I'm wondering: Who created this Burger King, anyway? Who created the "Burger Throne" on which he sits? Did a cartoonist think him up, or what?

OODLE-DOODLE!
OODLE-DOODLE!

Around 2 o'clock on Wednesday afternoon, O'Toole realized that he wanted to throw his iPhone into the Kalamazoo River.

Why? Let's face it: All O'Toole did anymore was sit around waiting for phone calls, text messages, emails, Tweets, Facebook updates, weather bulletins and Associated Press World News Headlines to come beeping across the infernal device –

But wait a minute... where, exactly, had that word "infernal" just come from?

Suddenly, O'Toole's blood ran cold. What if the goddam *Devil* had invented the iPhone in order to trick unwitting souls into a digital version of Hell? Come to think of it... that guy who owned Apple, the maker of the iPhone... but, hey, *wait just a damn minute*, wasn't the "Apple" exactly what the goddam Devil had presented to Eve in the Garden of Eden, way back when?

"Here... take a bite of *this* rascal – then you'll know as much as God does."

Holy-moly! And what about that Apple CEO, that really strange dude in the buzz-cut and the huge, perpetual grin... didn't that dude even *look* a little bit like Beelzebub, when all was said and done?

Sitting at a back table in the West Kalamazoo McDonald's, O'Toole warned himself: *You're thinking too much, bozo: knock it off!*

Five decades earlier, you see, while being educated by the Sisters of the Sacred Misery, O'Toole had learned that it was best to keep his thinking to a minimum. Why? It was simple: Bad things happened when O'Toole thought.

Frowning now, he took a bite of his Classic Home Style Ranch Chicken Club. In what remained of his mind's eye, he could so easily picture the splash (ker*plunk*!) his iPhone would make as it went into the river. And how good it would feel to imagine the shiny metal gizmo lying at the bottom of the watercourse with the AP World Headlines flickering uselessly across the slowly dying screen!

SCHWARZENEGGER TO MARRY HOUSEKEEPER

CLEMENS DENIES STEROID USE – AGAIN

STUDY: SOME DINOSAURS WERE SMALLER THAN CHICKENS

How wonderful it would be, O'Toole thought: *To be unreachable.*

The iPhone would *oodle-doodle* endlessly, way down there at the bottom of Kalamazoo's eponymous stream, and no one would ever answer!

Oodle-doodle!
Oodle-doodle!

But then, all at once, O'Toole's reverie was interrupted.

Ronald McDonald had just entered the eatery! White-faced and wearing enormous orange-plastic galoshes, the boisterous trademark was galumphing from one table to the next, shaking hands all around.

All too soon, the Mickey D clownster was in O'Toole's face.

"Hi, sir! How you been doing?"

O'Toole reflected for a moment. "I'm okay," he said. "Going pretty good."

Now the cerise-mouthed fast-food brand lifted both thumbs skyward in a gesture of all-out bonhomie. "That's cool," he sang. "That's cool as a tool!"

Then he headed for the next table.

"I'll become a Cistercian monk," O'Toole told himself. "First I'll throw my iPhone in the river. Then I'll wander deep into the woods… deep into that big woodsy area located just south of Kalamazoo.

"I'll find an old board-shack somebody abandoned back in the early 1990s, back when the cell phones were first coming in and the only way to go online was via dial-up."

A monk! He would sit in the board-shack at twilight listening to the evening's first whippoorwills, and he would work at not thinking. Alone in his board-shack, he would be freed forever from the brutal anxiety of waiting for that next summons from the Devil's own favorite high-tech device:

Oodle-doodle!
 Oodle-doodle!

BIRDS ARE DESCENDED
FROM DINOSAURS

Quinn went back to his boyhood parish – St. Anthony's of Buena Vista– in an effort to better understand the fires of Eternal Hell.

As a child in Buena Vista, Quinn had been taught that if he messed up, he would be tortured forever by shrieking demons armed with red-hot bars of superheated metal. Begging and crying would prove useless; once the horn-snouted devils had you in their grip, no power could save you.

Quinn checked into the EconoLodge on Highway 17, two miles south of Buena Vista. It was a mild summer afternoon, with lots of bird-chatter, and Quinn felt strangely euphoric. But he'd downed two shots of vodka at the Applebee's in Staunton, about an hour earlier, and he wondered if the shots explained the euphoria? Also, he distrusted that adverb – *strangely* – because he knew it could flip him into "a major-league anxiety attack," if he wasn't careful. (This was a phrase he'd used some years earlier, during his lengthy psychoanalysis with Dr. Zappala: "major-league anxiety attack.")

Now he looked out the window of EconoLodge Unit No. 224 and saw several robins working a 20-foot-long rectangle of bright green grass. They were hunters, no doubt about that. But also elegant – those orange-vested creatures owned a stern authority. Why? With a mild shock, Quinn suddenly remembered: Birds are descended from dinosaurs. Where had he learned that? *USA Today? Jurassic Park?*

The priest at St. Anthony's, a German-American from Ohio named Father Horstnagel, had taught Quinn that the Devil was endlessly clever and endlessly subtle. His game (the Devil's, that is) was to try and trick human souls into the "fiery pit," where he would then have license to torture them forever. (The torture would be his revenge for having been defeated by God in the cosmic struggle between good and evil.)

It was a lot for a seven-year-old to digest.

But Quinn had done his best.

According to Dr. Zappala, Father Horstnagel's teaching had resulted in some trauma, some lifelong confusion.

"It's like a computer," Dr. Z had said, somewhere near the middle of their second year of working together. "Garbage in, garbage out! The computer can only process the information it's been given, know what I mean?"

***

The next morning, bright and early, Quinn dropped by the old church in order to look at some historical records. Mrs. Blasingame, a parish volunteer, had agreed to show him four or five boxes of newspaper clippings and other memorabilia... after Quinn described himself on the phone as "an old Latin-spouting altar boy who's thinking about writing his autobiography."

Before breaking out the boxes, however, Mrs. Blasingame had taken Quinn on a quick tour of the church's recently restored Stations of the Cross.

"We sent them all the way to Rome," said the elderly volunteer, as the two of them stood beneath a gleaming, *bas*-relief panel on one side of the stone-walled nave. "These Stations were originally carved from pure ivory, and the restoration really brought them back to life!"

"I see what you mean," said Quinn. They were looking at Station No. 7 – *Jesus is Whipped in the Marketplace* – and Quinn was amazed by the naked ferocity of the whip-handlers.

"So vivid!" said Mrs. Blasingame.

After a few minutes she took Quinn down to a basement storeroom so that he could go through the boxes of old clippings and memorabilia.

He sat at a long, wooden table, obviously an antique, and for a few moments he wondered if this might be the same table where he'd learned about the Devil and his tricks, as a struggling and often fearful second-grader attending Saturday morning catechism classes.

Mrs. Blasingame patted his shoulder, "Happy research!" and padded off to resume her churchly duties.

Quinn spent the next couple of hours looking through faded St. Anthony Bulletins and occasional clips from the Buena Vista *Democrat* that described fund-raising projects and building additions over the years. It was pretty dull going for the most part: *Wednesday Night Bingo to Resume Sept. 14*, and Quinn felt himself slowly drifting away on a tide of flickering drowsiness....

But then, down near the bottom of the second box, his hand found an entire front page from the newspaper. Dated 20 years earlier, the lead-story on the page was headlined:

Former St. Anthony Pastor Perishes in Calif. House Fire

Lawrenceville, Calif. (AP) – *Father Willem Horstnagel, a former longtime pastor at St. Anthony Parish in Buena Vista, died during a predawn rectory fire in this small northern California town early Wednesday morning.*

Father Horstnagel, a Precious Blood father who had served as pastor at St. Anthony's for more than ten years during the 1960s and early 1970s, perished while trying to warn other residents to flee. The St. Jude Rectory in Lawrenceville burned to the ground.

Quinn read the brief news dispatch several times.

Then he replaced the clippings and church bulletins in their boxes. He thanked Mrs. Blasingame and departed the church. It was late morning by now, with a line of silver-black thunderheads approaching town from the Blue Ridge Mountains to the west.

Quinn drove slowly through Buena Vista. That old German priest had warned Quinn about the fires of Hell... and then he himself had died in the roaring flames of an all-consuming rectory fire!

Did it mean anything?

SOMETIMES MAKING SOMETHING LEADS TO NOTHING

Try as he might, O'Dell could not understand modern art. He was Irish, after all.

"Shit," said O'Dell. "What *is* this stuff?"

At the Baltimore Art Museum, O'Dell had spent more than an hour staring at a group of chicken claws nailed to a board. Some of the claws had bloodstains on them. Beside each claw hung a short length of rope. There was straw on the floor.

The artist had only one name, according to a flyer O'Dell had picked up in the museum lobby: BLOK.

That flyer also described the claws sculpture – *Hen, Woman, Rope* – as "an exploration of the female mythos of the Russian steppe."

O'Dell looked at all of this and he felt a thrill of fear. Who was BLOK, and why had she nailed those chicken claws to the gallery wall?

Try as he might, he simply couldn't grasp the meaning of it.

Deep down, O'Dell knew it would be pointless to ask anyone about the sculpture. How well he remembered the scorching humiliation he'd suffered ten years earlier, when he'd dared (at the end of a public lecture at The Johns Hopkins University School of the Humanities) to ask the world-renowned sculptor Christo why he'd wrapped one of the Florida Keys in Saran Wrap.

"Sir," O'Dell had wailed from his perch near the back of the hall, "wrapping that Key required huge amounts of Saran Wrap. What were you hoping to accomplish, exactly?"

Christo, who wore an enormous golden earring shaped like the sun, had sneered openly at the question.

"I do this thing," growled Christo, "for one reason and one reason only: I am *Christo*!"

Nodding agreement, the entire audience had turned to glare angrily at O'Dell.

Apparently, the big-time artists didn't want you to ask them any serious questions about their work.

Yes, asking questions of the big-time artists could get you in a whole lot of trouble, fast. On another occasion – thank God he'd kept his mouth shut that day! – a famous sculptor from New York had delivered a gallery talk about some pieces of felt that he'd smeared liberally with sheep fat. Asked what these *objets d'art* "represented," the felt-smearer had curled his upper lip: "Madame, they do not represent anything. They are what they are – and I sincerely hope that you are what *you* are!"

The questioner, obviously wiped out on the museum's $6.95-a-glass white wine, had slurred resentfully back at him: "Huuuuuuuuuhhh?"

The truth is that O'Dell had been thoroughly terrified by his infrequent encounters with modern art.

How well he remembered that afternoon at the Rijksmuseum 20 years before, when he'd spent nearly half an hour trying to "feel the vibes" from a transparent plastic sculpture shaped like a giant seashell. Nameless and unidentified, the *objet d'art* hung from a gallery wall, right inside the door... and O'Dell had asked himself long and hard why the curators had chosen to give it this position of prominence.

The answer came in the next gallery, when O'Dell discovered an exact replica of the "seashell" – and saw that it was full of flyers describing the art in that particular room.

O'Dell knew he was stupid. And yet he couldn't stop gnawing at the questions posed by modern art. That chicken-claw sculpture, for example – *Hen, Woman, Rope*: was it perhaps an attempt to somehow capture the soul of a chicken coop marooned on the steppes of Central Russia? Was *that* the point? According to the flyer, viewers were encouraged to "interact" with BLOK by sending her an email at blok@yahoo.com. But O'Dell was deathly afraid of looking dumb again, and it took him nearly a month to find the guts to compose an electronic message to the claw lady.

Finally, he managed to hit the "send" button, however.

"Dear BLOK: Caught your Claws in Baltimore, and just hoping to learn a bit more here about what they might mean. Have a nice weekend! O'DELL."

Several days passed with no reply. Then BLOK responded:

"Dear O'DELL: I suggest you Google this phrase: *sometimes making something leads to nothing.*"

O'Dell didn't hesitate. He quickly Googled *sometimes making something leads to nothing...* and he was amazed by what he found!

THE HALBERD-BEARER

He who is not busy being born is busy dying.
–Bob Dylan

Seated on a bench in the sunshine, Magoon reviewed his prospects.

A red-crested woodpecker clattered nearby.

"I'm fading fast," Magoon told himself. "Already, I resemble a character out of Beckett – one of those older guys who sits in the park at 3 p.m. and drools on his sleeve."

The woodpecker banged his head against the oak eight times in rapid succession.

"Must be Irish," thought Magoon. Or did he say it aloud?

Then he thought: "That's a very lively woodpecker, over there… but what about *my* pecker?"

No comment.

He shifted his buttocks on the bench. It was a mild summer afternoon. The birds were cavorting in the branches near Magoon's head, etc.

Magoon was 70.

He no longer bothered to review his life. Magoon had wasted 20 years in that pointless effort – before finally concluding (in the words of the great American philosopher Woody Allen): "I got screwed."

Hah-hah!

Magoon's mother, Mrs. Magoon, had once cracked a raw egg on her son's pate. "Ho!" Mrs. Magoon had roared as the slimy contents dribbled along her boy's nose: "Now the yolk's on *you*!"

He sighed, remembering that long-ago moment of connection between mother and son, and his jaw fell open. Now he yawned deeply. He yawned like an ancient, glaring, massively drugged water buffalo. Deep down, Magoon understood that he was a minor character. In Shakespearean parlance, he was a "halberd-bearer" – a guy who runs onstage with a metal-tipped pole in one hand. He stands there, blinking fast, for about 20 seconds. Then a trumpet blares three times in quick succession… and the halberd-bearer runs offstage, never to be seen again.

For a few moments, Magoon found himself wondering what the halberd-bearer did during the endless hours and weeks and months when he was offstage. Did he sit on a log at the edge of the forest with his gnarled hands folded neatly in his lap? Did he whistle a ditty or two, simply in order to fill up the time with some harmless ditty-whistling?

"I'm just a halberd-bearer...
Lugging around a metal lance;
I'm just a halberd-bearer...
Running errands for the Duke of France!"

Screwed!

"Let's face it, I'm trivial," thought Magoon. "I'm far too insignificant to be a major character in a Beckett drama. Hey, I'm just me, Magoon, sitting on a bench in the late-August sunshine."

He sighed. His dear mother, Mrs. Magoon, had long ago gone to her well-deserved reward. (And how long would it be before Magoon went to *his* well-deserved reward?)

But now he looked up; the red-crested woodpecker had returned to his oak.

Bap, bap, bap, *bap*, the bird pounded his head against the unyielding trunk. Magoon blinked slowly. Then he looked down at the brown paper bag in his left hand. That bag contained a tuna sandwich and two five-inch lengths of wilted celery.

Magoon deliberated. Should he eat his tuna sandwich here in the park, or back in his rented room?

TWO GUYS IN A CAR

The guy at the wheel, Clawson: "You want Dunkin' Donuts?"

The other guy, Bud: "Naw. Get some if you want. Not me."

Clawson: "What's the prob?"

Bud: "Heart attack in a box."

Clawson: "Get real."

Bud: "I saw a health thing on Katie Couric. Guy ate a jelly doughnut, his blood turned all milky-white with cholesterol."

The car is a green Datsun. It's Clawson's. He's got a fuzzy monkey hanging from the rearview mirror. The monkey's grinning big-time. He's truly happy. He's jiggling on his string as the Datsun swings left onto Howard.

"Fuck you, you too good for Dunkin' Donuts," says Clawson.

"No, listen," says Bud. "Get some. It don't matter to me."

"Let's finish the job," says Clawson. "Then we eat."

"Okey-doker," says Bud. "What's the deal, Mr. Claw?"

"The usual," says Clawson. "We just walk into his office, we tell him we represent Mr. Stein. He takes care of business, everything is copasetic. If not... we do some persuading. We bend his fingers a little. Nothing terminal."

"What's his name?" asks Bud.

"You know I can't tell you that."

"You're carrying, aren't you?"

"Not your concern, Bud."

"Why you carrying, this ain't terminal?"

Clawson's face lights up in a huge grin. His teeth are large and yellow. For a moment, he looks a bit like the jiggling monkey. Big yellow grin, big blunt teeth gleaming in the rearview mirror.

"Soupy Sales is dead," he says. "Died yesterday."

"Pardon?" says Bud.

"That comic? The guy used to take all those pies in the face? Hah-hah! He's doing a standup routine... little old lady runs onstage carrying a shaving cream pie. Whap! Whap! Funny shit! You ask too many questions, Bud. Just settle back. We go in, we say hello, we explain how we represent Mr. Stein. He takes care of business, everything is copasetic. Huh? Huh?"

"All right," says Bud. "Listen, we can do Dunkin' Donuts, if you want."

"Naw. That's fine. We're past it now."

The green Datsun turns onto the southbound ramp of I-95.

"I like slapstick," says Clawson. "The Stooges? Huh? You got one Stooge slapping the dogshit out of the *other* Stooge – three really funny fuckers, and which one is it makes that little screaming sound?"

"Couldn't say, Mr. Claw."

"I think it's Moe. Is it Moe? Every time he gets slapped, he makes this little screaming sound. Huh? And he wears this wig. Curly slaps him so hard the wig flies off, and he makes this little screaming sound. Or they try to paint a room, and Curly swings the paint brush and it hits Moe in the face. And then he steps in the paint can. Now he can't get the can off his foot... he's hopping around the room with paint all over his face, and his foot's stuck in the can! Hah!"

They're surrounded by semi-trucks now. They're rolling south, semis all around them. The truck tires are howling as they blast down the asphalt at 70 miles an hour. "Soupy Sales is dead," saysClawson.

"All right," says Bud. "I hear you."

SUMMER GHOST, NAG'S HEAD

Three p.m. The white eye of the sun hangs motionless over the dunes.

Not a breath of air.

The surf tumbles onto the sand. The surf retreats. The surf tumbles onto the sand.

Sombody's portable radio: "Ten past three, and 94 degrees in downtown Nag's Head. Time for some more music. Here come the Everly Brothers – *never knew what I missed, until I kissed ya!*"

We were out of money, so we decided to hike the dunes. Kill some time. Teenagers on a summer afternoon, you know? When you're out of money, and time is all you own?

So we're drifting along, three boys in ratty sneakers.

If you listen carefully, you can hear the wind pushing the grains of sand. It's a tiny sound, whispers in your ear: *Ssshhhhhhhh... sleeping!*

The sun doesn't move.

The surf tumbles onto the beach. "Hey, look up there," says Doyle. "What *is* that wreck, anyway? Abandoned house? Looks like part of the roof caved in. Come on!"

We're amazed. This falling-down house in the middle of the dunes – how'd it get here? Why hasn't it been torn down? Does anybody know it's here? Painted a dull-ass green... paint flaking... warped shingles... windows all smashed out.

The three of us creep up to the ruined front door. Three kids, each 15. We're way back in the 1950s, in this story. We can't see you. You can't touch us. The words on this page – no other way to reach us. Hello from 1959!

"What a dump," says Tyler.

"Let's check it out," says Doyle.

We push through the buckled doorway. The front room... dead spiders. And it's crawling with shadows. Light spooling through the busted window frames. "Spooky as shit," says Doyle. Me, I'm just standing there, wondering what everything is. When you're 15? The days come and go, and the waves creep over the bright sand.

A second door. A bedroom? It's stuck... we have to work to get it open. The floor is gone back here, nothing but white sand underfoot, and you can see how the dune is gradually swallowing the house. Nothing lasts forever, right? That summer wind, hissing through the frames – a few grains of sand trickle down the slope. Come back in 20 or 30 years and you'll be lost. The dune will have moved on you; the town will have shifted half a mile to the west.

Never knew what I missed –

So we're fooling around in this back room. One piece of furniture – an old rocking chair, one arm splintered. Dead brown wood. Doyle climbs aboard, rocks awkwardly back and forth. "Say hello to yer old grandmaw!"

But we don't laugh. Too weird. Doyle eyeballs us for a second. "Okay, here's a dare," he says. "Two of us will leave, go outside, and the third one has to stay in here alone – for at least five minutes. Bet you two don't have the balls."

"You're on," I say. "I'll go first."

I follow them out to the smashed front door. I watch them walk over the grassy shoulder of the nearest dune. I'm alone now. The sunlight is so intense it looks blue against the sand....

I turn back into the wrecked house.

I'm alone in the heat. So hot, it's murder. What's that smell? Tar boiling on the roof? I take a few steps toward the bedroom. What's that crunching underfoot? Okay, broken glass. I'm walking –

Hold it –

Beat-up old rocking chair, and now a woman in it.

The roots of my scalp go electric, and I make a gasping sound like I've been slugged in the gut.

"Ma'am?"

No reply. Tiny thing, white hair tucked under a soiled kerchief. One eyelid sagging. Wet blue gaze.

"Ma'am?"

When she speaks, it's a groaning sound. Barely audible. No louder than the summer wind going through the dune grasses: "Say hello to yer old grandmaw!" I'm staring at her. Isn't that what Doyle said? Weren't those Doyle's words, exactly?

"Ma'am," I tell her. "Ma'am, I'm sorry. We were fooling around in the dunes." I can hear the roof ticking in the heat. The waves tumble onto the sand.

Then I surprise myself. "Ma left us!" I blurt at her. "She walked out on us, last December. Have *you* seen her, maybe?"

No reply. The rocker doesn't budge.

But her eyes are moving. They're all over me. I'm afraid to ask her my next question, but I know I must.

"Ma'am, are you a ghost?"

She sends me a thin, thin smile. She holds out one small, pale, nearly translucent hand. I take it. That hand is light as the wind, fleet as the summer wind in the dune grasses.

"Do you know what we are, sonny? Do you know what we really are? We're sunlight, and we're shadows running across the sand. You let her go, do you hear me? You let that shadow go!"

I look down, my hand is empty.

The empty rocker quivers for a moment, then goes still.

The other two – they're already banging through the door. Hollering. "Bet you shit yourself in here alone, didn't you!"

What am I going to tell them?

A MYSTERY STORY
IN 22 PARAGRAPHS

A March afternoon. The gunmetal clouds throw themselves around the sky... there's a fat one, baggy, sliding toward the crest of the hill –

And you're asking: Do men have souls?

Here at Holy Redeemer Cemetery on the east side of Crabtown –

Yes, look into his eye: the stalked, shuddering eye of the crab, on this wet... beneath this gelid rain-wave: March in Crabtown: somehow your steps have carried you to this cemetery on the east side of town, you should be in your office, you should be working –

But you read online somewhere a fragment from St. Augustine: *Love God and do as you wish....*

What the crab knows: he knows how to wait, while the bleached-white limestone seeps micron by micron into his shell and micron by micron *becomes* that shell: and then his eye on its stalk can *ride* that shell, observing, observing:

What I saw that day at the Cem...

An old man in a tattered coat, a greenish raincoat... spiky white hair like white barbed wire licking from beneath his bent hat –

His eye a lozenge of blue in his twisting head

He's watching me, I'm watching him.

"What's your game?" I asked myself. "You're sneaking about this graveyard! You're after something; anyone can see you're a creature straight out of Balzac. Your red nose, your sharp sharp nose – you won't fool me, you sneak!"

I'm watching him from the corner of one eye. Have you seen those March afternoons when the clouds bulge grotesquely, the color of faded lead – then a quick... spatter – your face is suddenly wet, you shiver: a live being, caught on the edge of a frozen hook, twisting?

And so I watched him creep up to a headstone. He slipped the damp blossoms from beneath his arm... he fed them into a dull green vase at the foot of the grave –

He looked around furtively –

He approached the blunt square chiseled monument, the soiled gray heft of it, another poor bastard trying to escape his fate with an incantation: *Blessed be those who are poor in spirit –*

And I watched him bend from the waist and I watched him sneak a look to be sure no one could see him

(but I was hidden among branches)

and he kissed that cold dead stone.

He kissed her gravestone!

I saw it. I swear it.

That day.

The mystery of it... in a world where... you can love God... and you can... *do as you wish!*

DAMAGED FRUIT

What is life? What is fate? Why does the air keep leaking out of your right rear tire?

Dolan could not answer these questions.

Increasingly, he had begun to suspect that he was simply a computer-based simulation of a human being that had been created by a future civilization.

I do feel digital, Dolan told himself. Shit, I'm probably just part of a video game some kid is playing in 2816.

He reached for a purple plum, intent on squeezing it... but his hand-eye coordination had been eroding with the years—*Jesus*, there went the cantaloupes!

Fourteen of them were now rolling merrily along the floor of the Super Fresh!

Standing nearby, the simulated produce manager – his name tag said "Willard" – scowled fiercely at Dolan. All at once the computer-based simulation tasted fear. It tasted like the green mold that grows on ancient, simulated pennies.

"I'm... accident!" croaked Dolan.

He knelt and began to retrieve the bruised melons.

"I'll handle it," growled Willard. "You have yourself a nice day."

Dolan rose from his knees. He was awash in simulated guilt. How could he explain to this irked factotum that both of them were merely electronic streams rushing along some 14-year-old's flickering web browser in 2816?

"Willard," he wanted to say. "I was a Catholic altar boy once. *Introibo ad Altare Dei*! But I wasn't a *real* altar boy; I was only a simulated altar boy. And when Father Horstnagel said *Dominus Vobiscum*... we're talking 1s and 0s here, my man. That *Dominus Vobiscum* of his was a series of data-bits, and nothing more.

"He was an algorithm, Willard – a wave of electrical energy winking along a silicon grid."

But the produce manager had turned away by now. Ignoring Dolan, he was re-stacking the damaged fruit.

Shaking his head mournfully, the cyber-ghost wandered down Aisle No. 8 and picked up three cans of Chicken of the Sea tuna, a plastic fly swatter and a box of Brillo pads for the simulated kitchen's pots and pans. In the background, the simulated Muzak system played a syrupy version of Carole King's classic 1971 hit, *You're So Far Away*.

He paid and left. Climbing behind the wheel of the Chevy Sprint, he groaned with pain – his simulated arthritis was acting up again, and he could feel it at work on his digitalized knee cartilage.

He turned the key in the ignition and the Chevy made a low-pitched, moaning sound... followed by a series of loud clicks. Dolan said: "Start, you sonofabitch."

He could imagine the 16-year-old cackling with laughter, way up in 2816, then barking at a pal: "Look here, this bozo's old tire-crawler just went dead on him!"

He drove slowly along Baltimore Avenue. It was a cloudless simulated autumn afternoon in 2011, and digital maples glowed softly beneath the simulated October sunshine.

"Oh, shit!" The Margie simulation had asked him to pick up a stick of simulated butter... and he'd forgotten completely about it!

TINY GILDERSLEEVE

Somewhere in the middle of April, Clancy began to pick up radio broadcasts in his dental fillings. The broadcasts had originally occurred 60 years before, when Clancy was in the second grade.

Deep inside one of Clancy's molars, a teensy radio voice wailed: "*Leeee*-roy! Stop it! Stop it now!"

Listening to his tooth-radio, Clancy nearly crapped himself.

That was the voice of *The Great Gildersleeve*! And *Leeee*-roy was his orphaned nephew. *Leeee*-roy was his ten-year-old nemesis. Was Gildersleeve the mayor of their town? No... he was the water commissioner. The radio played downstairs... the big Philco with the glowing tubes. Clancy had been "tucked in" for the night. He was 7.

He was 7.

The full moon hung in the window –

Clancy had been "tucked in." The moon was a fat gold coin, hanging. The tree branch on the other side of the glass was a gnarled arm, a skeletal arm reaching for him.

That was 1949.

But *this* was 2011.

How could a radio program from 60 years ago be playing inside his tooth? Was that really possible? Yes... Clancy had read somewhere (*USA Today*?) about people who could pick up radio signals in their fillings. It was physics, that's all. The electrons were drawn into the silver and gold; they swarmed inside the tooth and the eardrum converted that swarming into a micro-radio show –

Brought to you by Parkay Margarine... now you can buy it in a golden-yellow, quarter-pound stick!

"Hi, Unk! Can I have a quarter?"

"Now, *Leeee*-roy, I already gave you your allowance, and you know it. Why, I gave you 50 cents just yesterday!"

Clancy had been tucked in.

Outside the window, a black shadow skimmed along the white-painted clapboard.

That would be the night owl with the eyes of liquid gold.

That was the night owl, soundless in his flight –

But then a thought occurred to Clancy: that radio program, *The Great Gildersleeve*, wasn't actually playing inside his fillings – it was playing inside his *head*. It was flickering from one brain cell to the next.

Brought to you by Parkay Margarine!

And did it really matter if the radio program was playing in his fillings or in his head? Here was the Water

Commissioner, Gildersleeve... and here was his nephew, the pesky *Leeee*-roy

(what a word, thought Clancy: *pesky*)

And what were they, really?

Why, they were electrons! And did it really matter, in the final analysis, if they'd been hatched in a neighbor-galaxy? Did it matter if the micro-Gildersleeve had actually been created on a back street in Spiral Andromeda?

That mustache of his... that jet-black carpet-sweeper mustache: Clancy had merely imagined it. In reality, there *was* no mustache: it had been invented by the writers who'd created the radio show. Why, Gildersleeve himself had been invented by the writers who'd created the radio show!

And now he was alive again. Now he was living inside a filling in Clancy's jaw.

Or maybe inside his head?

In the final analysis, Gildersleeve was a phantom. He carried a forest-green umbrella in one hand, and that umbrella was made of electrons, and that umbrella had been created by the writers who'd written the radio show.

There *was* no Gildersleeve.

Tucked in for the night, Clancy listened to the Philco cabinet radio playing downstairs.

Deep inside those gold-glowing tubes, deep inside his nest of flickering electrons, tiny Gildersleeve pointed the green umbrella at his teensy nephew.

Leeee-roy!

AMONG THE OJIBWAS

Coughlin got loose at the Gun Lake Casino, and he soon became a pest. For starters, he went up to an elderly woman who was playing a *Buckin' Bronc!* five-cent slot-machine and pulled on her arm.

Then he blared at the startled recreational gambler: "Do you have red hair?"

She glared back at him. "Do you have a problem, sir?"

"I want a free drink of whiskey," said Coughlin. "Will you get it for me?"

The gambler-lady had heard enough. She'd been losing nickels all afternoon, and she wasn't about to be harassed by this senile dipstick. Fortunately, there was a small red "Security" button on the bottom of her slot machine. She hit it… and within half a minute, an Ojibwa gentleman named Charles Whitefeather was standing by her side.

"Good afternoon, ma'am," said Charles Whitefeather. "Is there an issue?"

"You bet there's an issue," said the gambler-lady. She jerked a thumb at Coughlin. "This asshole wants a free drink, and I'm supposed to get it for him."

Whitefeather gave the intruder a sweet, kiss-your-butt smile. "Sir," he said, "if all you need is a drink, I'll be happy to provide it for you. What say we head on up to the Four-Leaf Clover Lounge, and you can wet your whistle on the house?"

But Coughlin shook his head at the casino factotum.

"I think this woman has red hair," he announced, "and I don't like your pony tail worth a shit, either."

Whitefeather's eyes widened slightly. But he had seen many unnerving things as a member of the Gun Lake security staff, and he wasn't about to be thrown for a loop by a senile retiree who obviously belonged at Tender-Care.

"Tell you what," he crooned at the jut-jawed septuagenarian. "Instead of a whiskey-drink, how about some soft ice cream? We're a casino – there's no getting around that fact – but we also happen to make the best soft ice cream inWest Michigan, and you can quote me on that."

Coughlin listened to all of this carefully. Then he cocked his head to one side like a tropical bird responding to an unfamiliar sound-cue. "Here's a question for you," he said to the casino guard, "and I hope you're man enough to answer it: Are you one of the Indians who own this place?"

Whitefeather thought for a moment. Then: "I do belong to the Ojibwa Nation. But I just work here. I'm not too high on the totem pole, hah-hah!"

But now the irked slot-machine player broke in. "I don't mind if you two have a gab session," she glowered, "but I'm trying to win a jackpot here. Do you mind?"

Whitefeather nodded. "Absolutely," he said. "We're going for soft ice cream."

"No, we're not," said Coughlin. "Are you going to let this old bag push you around? What happened to the fighting spirit of Geronimo, anyway?"

Whitefeather showed no expression. "That was another tribe," he said. "Sir, I'm going to have to ask you to move along and let this lady play her game in peace."

Before Coughlin could respond to this, however, they were joined by a bouncy, middle-aged woman in a Chicago Cubs sweatshirt. "Hi, guys! I'm Kelly," boomed the new arrival. "Don't worry – he's my dad!"

Whitefeather blinked at her. "This gentleman is your father?"

"Co-rect. He got away from me, that's all. Trust me: he's harmless."

"The hell I am," said Coughlin.

"Is this a family convention, or what?" said the gambler-lady. "I didn't come here to be part of Old Home Week."

"Understood," said Coughlin's daughter. "No problema. We'll be moseying along from here, pronto."

"Let me tell you something," said Coughlin to Whitefeather. "I don't think you're much of an Indian, okay?"

"Dad!"

"It's okay," said Whitefeather. He turned to Kelly: "I understand that your dad has some issues, and that's fine.

I offered him some soft ice cream, but he wasn't interested."

"Am I going to have to call *another* security guard?" asked the gambler-lady.

"No, no," said Whitefeather. "We're out of here." To Kelly he said: "If you two will follow me up to customer-service, I have a small gift for you."

Coughlin snorted. "I don't take gifts from Comanches."

"Dad!"

But at least they were moving now. Scowling, the gambler-lady watched them depart. Then she pulled the handle... and won $217 by lining up three blazing six-shooters in a row!

DOWN ON THE
SOUTH SKUNK RIVER

I went back, first time in 25 years. One of those drowsy summer afternoons, mid-August, you remember? The black fly on the table – he's so fat he can barely waddle over to the blob of spilled grape jelly and start lapping.

Hello, fly.

Right here in this kitchen – my old daddy's big right hand would come up.

Those afternoons when he'd been down to Casey's? He smelled of burnt-tar and sugar-syrup, after Casey's. Smelled like the wet leaking out of a swollen peach, golden-red-ripe and bursting with the sweetness of late summer in Iowa.

Swack! – the meat of his hand going into the bridge of my nose. "You little shit!" Now I've got red-points, fire-points winking through my field of vision. I'm blinking. Trying not to bawl. I'm looking at the flecks of silver in his jaw-stubble. At Casey's, and also in town, they knew him as "C.J." They'd all be sitting together at one of the back tables... half of them wearing John Deere caps, and they're listening to a smutty story being told by the Ralston Purina salesman, Theo Box.

Haw!

C.J. slaps the table. "You oughta go on TV, Theo!"

I don't know what was wrong with him. Never did know. He had some kind of black hatred eating in his chest. I used to picture it... like a black spider in there, fangs going in and out of his heart-muscle.

He got the cancer about two years after I left for Des Moines and got my first job managing produce at the Family Fare Market. I'm stacking lettuce and tomatoes all afternoon... he's dying in the little blue house high up the bank of the South Skunk River. They buried him in the little Methodist Cemetery over in Story City.

It's funny, the things you remember. After I'd gone to bed, one eye swollen a little but no big deal, I'd listen to the two of them shouting at each other.

She's yelling: "You have no right. You have no *right*!"

"Get off my back, you stupid bitch!"

I'm listening to the frogs down on the river: gracka-gracka-*grack*.

As rivers go, the South Skunk wasn't very impressive. More like a creek – a 30-foot-wide thread of dark water curling beneath the town bridge. The fish were small, bony things... stunted bluegill, a few minor-league yellow perch. And the minnows flashing in the shallows, like a handful of flung dimes.

When I was in grade school, I spent a lot of time down by the river. I liked the smell, that mud-stink rising in the heat, and the musky aroma of rotting logs. I liked to imagine the troll who lived beneath the mossy stones of the bridge. A little old guy with a pretzel-bent spine and greenish bumps riding his nose....

    I don't blame C.J much. Not anymore. With the years, I've come to see that he was the prisoner of something invisible. Something I'll never know about. A force. A dark thing, maybe unknowable, like that spider I used to imagine at work on his heart.

BIG AL'S MOMENT OF COMPASSION

In those days, 20 years ago, I flipped burgers at Big Al's in the Columbia Mall.

My grammaw was dying, and she seemed very busy with that.

We served French fries in these little wax-paper envelopes with Big Al's printed on the side. The letters were bright red... so red that it could hurt your eyes to look at them.

One afternoon – I was 23 – I must've looked at the letters too hard, because I started to cry. I could see my grammaw's head on the pillow. I saw how wispy her hair had become; I saw it in my mind. I thought gossamer, and I imagined a few of those hairs floating in the light. Then the red letters jumped out at me, Big Al's, and I slowly came back to myself.

And there he was – standing right beside me and holding a box of Morton's salt.

"What's the matter, Sarah?"

Startled, I just gaped at him. Big Al was a fat Italian with three chins and a tattoo of a green lizard on his left forearm. His actual name was Allan Bonfadini, and he was in his eighth year of selling burgers and fries at Columbia Mall.

"Well... " I said. My mouth hung open – and all at once I made this really strange gurgling sound, like a fish trying to spit out a toxic worm or something. (You should know that I had dropped out of the University of Maryland a few months before, and I was now living in my mother's basement. Things had slowed way down for me. Did I even have a future? It was hard to say.)

"How come... why the tears?" said Big Al. "You got a problem with a boyfriend?"

I shook my head at this. Good God, boyfriend issues were the last thing I needed, right then.

"My grammaw Ellen," I told Al. "She's got cancer, see? She's fading pretty quickly... she's been through a lot."

He didn't say anything, just kept looking at me quietly.

"I'm all right," I said after a bit. I felt embarrassed because I could feel some wetness leaking out of one nostril.

"Listen here," said Al. "Everybody has a tough day now and then, know what I mean?"

I blinked at him.

"Tell you what."

He took a few steps to his left, over to the big nickel-plated cash register. He hit a key and the cash-drawer whanged open.

"You take this," he said.

I stared at his hand, which now held a $20 bill.

"What?" I said. "Money?"

"Movie," he said. "Jurassic Park – it's running every thirty minutes or so, right down there at Cinema Two. My treat.

"Get yourself some popcorn, a soda. Settle back and take it easy for a couple hours. Enjoy the show. My treat."

He waved toward the hamburger grill and the deep-fat fryer at the back of the fast-food stand.

"Slow day," he said. "Monday – what the hell, I can handle everything until Joey gets here at six."

***

What can I tell you?

I walked the mall for a few minutes, and then I went to Jurassic Park.

I didn't feel much better, as I watched the dinosaurs scream and attack, but the show did take my mind off those gossamer hairs floating in the pale light of grammaw's sick room.

What I remember most about that afternoon was the peaceful, echoing vastness of the nearly deserted mall. The strangeness of it, you know? That other-worldly look on the faces of the clothes mannequins at Forever 21?

Walking through the baked-dough aroma of Auntie Anne's Pretzels, I felt the cold emptiness of the life I'd been leading until then. And I saw – as I approached the cashier's window at Cinema Two – that I would have to learn how to take better care of myself in the days ahead.

STILL LIFE WITH DUNG BEETLE

Why doesn't the dung beetle revolt? Why doesn't he simply abandon his ball of shit and relocate to Carmel-by-the-Sea?

He's a spunky little guy. Legs never stop moving. Rolling that dung ball of his across the Big KMart parking lot. Look at those legs go. Shaping and reshaping his wheel of excrement, his legs flicker so busily, and he's doing just fine, hey, it's Wednesday afternoon, about four o'clock, and he's telling himself: *Don't forget – PTA meeting tomorrow night.*

But then he yanks himself to a stop. Oh, boy – he forgot to mail in the insurance premium.

What if he bites the dust and there's no money for burial?

The scientists know why he pushes that dung ball. They say he's "coded" for it. The code was written eons earlier, they say, deep in the ancestor-deoxyribonucleic acid that evolved into the dung beetle's cellular protein. It just happened, apparently. The sun came up, minnows darted through the shallows, and the pond bubbled happily as the dung beetle's ancestor-deoxyribonucleic acid cooked in the soft, butter-yellow sunlight.

But the beetle doesn't know any of this. All he knows is that when he sees that shit ball, he wants to push it. And he does. He pushes it back and forth across the Big KMart parking lot. He never stops to ask himself Philosophical Question No. 23: "If the world consists entirely of appearances – ice melts to water boils to gas – then how shall we define 'reality?'"

Is it all flux – nothing more than *flux*?

And if it's all *flux*… well, does it really matter if he's nothing more than a scrabbling dung beetle?

Back and forth across the Big KMart parking lot. Gotta keep a low profile… lest he end his dung-pushing days as lunch for one of those bullet-headed Lake Michigan seagulls!

Things are, that's all. We're here. Do you think the dung beetle frets when he comes upon a torn paper cup lying in his path? Do you think he torments himself because he can't read the word printed in bright green on the side of that cup?

DIXIE.

For the dungster, it's *all* hieroglyph. The warm puddle, the sun-bright asphalt, the distant rain shower pattering on the pale blue hills above the town: Is there a connection between these familiar things and DIXIE?

Why ask? Time to get moving again. The dung beetle squares his shoulders, takes a deep breath. And soon he's hustling along the parking lot, pushing and pulling at his rough globe of pungent waste. Skinny legs flicker, flicker as he perpetually shapes his crap wheel, rolls it through the world from one yawning minute to the next.

He's coded, you see? You'll find him at twilight on the steep side of Norristown Hill. Taking a breather. Waiting patiently for darkness, so he can burrow under a leaf and rest his weary paws.

His shit-stained paws.

Will a marauding bat find him tonight?

Will it all end in a blur of agonizing pain, a split-second vision of closing needle-teeth?

Probably not.

He'll probably awaken at dawn, and stretch his cramped legs. Groan once or twice.

Start pushing.

THIS IS A RED LINE TRAIN TO HOWARD

My friend Al was dead.

I'd just come from the funeral home.

Pumphrey Brothers. I'd listened to the organ tones and I'd inhaled the sickly-sweet odor of roses, lilies and violets.

Al's face had seemed much smaller than I remembered. His mouth was pale orange and thin as a blade. One eyebrow stuck up a little where the adhesive had apparently failed.

He was gone. Now the subway car rumbled north. On the other side of the window, the Chicago streets crawled with late-afternoon traffic. Taillights flared like red-hot coals at the intersections. From time to time a loudspeaker crackled to life somewhere above our heads: *This is a Red Line train to Howard.*

Al had poured beer on his head once.

It happened on the boardwalk at Ocean City.* Some college girl was throwing a party out front of Polock Johnny's. Pitchers of beer... and a neon sign kept flickering on and off: *Biggest Dog On The Beach!* Al was holding a plastic cup full of Budweiser; in a flash, he was pouring the icy brew onto his head! And he was shouting in a drunken slur: "Hey! Hey! I just don't give a royal rat's ass!"

That crazy, crazy guy.

He ran the Tugboat Willie ride, that summer.

All day long, buckling the kiddies into the little tugboats. Then reaching for the big black switch on the wall of the maintenance shed. The gears crunch, the cable jerks a couple of times, and off they go.

You wake up one morning and you realize that those summers were forty years ago. The way that hot orange light fell on the foot-worn boards. The surf whispering at the edge of the sand. All day the carnival music bleats from the yellow calliope parked beside Sizzlin' Boardwalk Fries!

Daisy, Daisy, give me your answer, please....

At night fiery sparks jet from the rails beneath the Crack-the-Whip. The sea breeze cruises among the plastic pennants out front of *Big League Hurler – Try Your Luck!* You think it's going to last forever, but it doesn't.

It does not.

And the strangeness everywhere: That blue shadow inching away from the leg of the picnic table, as the long afternoon slowly advances.

I didn't touch him. I could have slipped one hand into the casket; I could have grazed his pale, faintly blue chin.

But I didn't want to feel that cold. I knew his skin would feel damp, chilled. No thanks.

Later, years after that summer, I asked him: "Al, why'd you pour the beer on your head that day?"

He blinked and frowned... didn't answer me.

"Hey! Hey! I just don't give a royal rat's ass!"

Life goes on. You look across the aisle; the fat girl in the *White Sox* sweatshirt has fallen asleep. Her head jerks sideways as we hit a curve. She opens one eye for a moment –

"This is a Red Line train to Howard."

---

*Ocean City, 1964. Summertime population: 84,500. Length of resort boardwalk: 2.9 miles.

GETAWAY!

One window. Rain slopping down the glass. Valdez lay on the bed in room 220 of the Lazy Acres Motel. He had five more hours to kill.

They weren't going to hit the bank in Chanute until 5 p.m. Closing time.

Valdez had the remote in his hand. He clicked on "Power," and the TV screen lit up. Channel 16: *Cooking With Quinn*. Fine. Valdez liked these cooking shows... they soothed him. He admired the way the big-time chefs sliced their vegetables. In the hands of a big-time chef, the chopping looked like magic. The knife became a blur, and the big yellow onion instantly transformed itself into a neat pile of identical slices.

That was precision. Valdez was a fan of precision.

The three of them had the routine down perfectly.

Exactly 120 seconds inside the bank... and then you're jumping into the car. Drive one mile and switch vehicles. By nightfall they'd be in Arkansas, laughing together over their Bud Lites.

But then he looked up from Quinn... the window had just flashed. He watched a second white scribble run down the panes... and he braced for the thunder. But it was far off, just a low rumble like an empty barrel rolling down the cellar stairs.

Quinn was sautéing a couple of garlic cloves in his cast iron pan.

Valdez closed his eyes. Funk and Moody would be leaving Wichita about now. He pictured the two of them sitting in the Dodge pickup. Funk would be at the wheel, his chocolate-brown fedora pulled down low to keep the July sun off his face. Moody would be eating from a cellophane bag with a monocle-wearing peanut-guy on it. Planter's. Valdez was on the edge of dozing....

They were fifteen miles down the Interstate when Moody spotted the blue flasher. Kansas State Trooper. "Fuck. Fuck! You gotta pull over," Moody told Funk.

Funk's eyes were huge. The three guns were in the trunk, hidden inside a bag full of golf clubs.

"Jesus," said Funk. "What if he searches the bag, Moody?"

"We ain't got a choice," said Moody. "Pull over."

Valdez opened one eye. How long had he been dozing? Quinn had vanished from the TV screen; now some college girls were playing volleyball on a beach somewhere. Valdez yawned. He needed to take a leak.

The Strangeness

There was a raggedy-ass paperback on the top of the toilet. Valdez picked it up. The cover showed two desperate-looking men inside a Dodge pickup truck. The windshield had been blasted out and the truck was careening along on two wheels, looking as if it might tip over at any minute.

The name of the book was: ***Getaway!***

Valdez finished his leak. He carried the book back to the bed. Idly, he flipped to the last page, the last paragraph:

Suddenly, a shadow fell against the motel room window. Two shadows. Two men, their weapons drawn, were approaching the door of 220. They wore identical-looking Smokey Bear hats. Cops? State Troopers? All at once Valdez knew he had a choice to make. Give up... or run? Surrender... or fight? He rose from the bed. His right hand went to where his shoulder holster should have been. But his gun was in the pickup truck. What to do? He stood frozen beside the bed, listening to the sound of knuckles against his door.

Valdez stopped reading. He was amazed. The guy in the story... *he's got my name! Valdez!*

He flipped back to the cover: ***Getaway!***

Then he turned to the first page, and he read the opener:

One window. Rain slopping down the glass. Valdez lay on the bed in room 220 of the Lazy Acres Motel. He had five more hours to kill....

COMFORTING MR. T

I can tell you about a moment in time, onrushing time –

About Mr. T, the owner and operator of Mr. T's Grocery on 29th Street. One of those little sawed-off guys, those wizened guys –

This city is full of them. They run the corner groceries; they stand all day long behind the fly-specked glass shelves. They wear suspenders and they sell Atomic Fireballs for ten cents each.

One thin dime.

And so I says to Mr. T: "How you doing?" And he's got this little cigarette butt poking from between his gray-fleshed lips. He's standing there behind the candy counter on 29th Street… a late-summer afternoon, a trapezoid of burnt-orange sunlight flickering against the worn floorboards of his little store –

Car radio goes by: *Never knew what I missed… until I kissed ya!*

And Mr. T's blinking at me through his owl-specs, and his wet green eyes are jiggling behind the specs –

"How you doing, Mr. T?"

And then I try to show him... I try to let him know I understand that The Mrs. is dying in the back room. I want him to know I understand she's dying of cancer back there, but I don't want to hurt him. Huh? I don't want to hurt him, so I just say:

"How's The Mrs. holding up, Mr. T?"

The green eyes quiver behind the owl-specs.

He says: "Awww... pretty much holding her own."

I nod. "Good," I tell him. "That's good."

Do you know what this is?

This is an August afternoon in Crabtown, with the heat soaking into us like scalding oil.

A pigeon, look at him, scrabbling around in the gutter for a watermelon seed.

A big orange billboard across the street, bent tin, hanging slant above the doughnut joint: NEHI. A few doors down, the red-clay bricks of the Greek Orthodox Church are baking patiently in the yellow glare....

Nothing moves....

And everything is rushing past.

The church bricks are baking, and suddenly you want to shout: "Come down here and *be* this agony, the agony in Mr. T's back room! Come down and watch Mr. T stub out his little smoke in the chipped glass ashtray!"

It's a moment, that's all.

He takes the limp dollar bill you hand him, deposits it in the frayed cigar box marked *Receipts*.

Gives you back a dime and a penny.

You look at him for a moment. A little guy in a dirty yellow smock. A German? A Czech? And The Mrs. dying slowly in the back room. In Crabtown, the east side, the year is 1980 – and you're standing there holding a sweating bottle of RC Cola and you want to shout at him: "Here we are, Mr. T! Here we are... alive!"

But it's just another day.

You can't shout that.

You say: "Hang in there, Mr. T."

He says: "Will do."

Now look over there, against that dusty plate-glass window, look at that fat black fly drugged with the late-summer sweetness, nosing against the scrap of newsprint stuck in that window-crack –

Look at that ragged nose of his going up against the capital-letter "E" in a word in a newsprint headline:

"DIES"

    Bzzzzt!

Bzzzzt!

Summer. Mr. T. RC Cola. The Mrs. dying in the back room.

The increasingly befuddled but laughter-loving author of *The Strangeness* resides in Hastings, Michigan. You can reach him at tomnugent@sbcglobal.net, should you have a question that isn't answered for you in this volume.

Made in the USA
Lexington, KY
22 December 2011